THY ROD AND THY STAFF

Other Books by Debbie Viguié

The Psalm 23 Mysteries

The Lord is My Shepherd
I Shall Not Want
Lie Down in Green Pastures
Beside Still Waters
Restoreth My Soul
In the Paths of Righteousness
For His Name's Sake
Walk Through the Valley
The Shadow of Death
I Will Fear No Evil
Thou Art With Me

The Kiss Trilogy

Kiss of Night
Kiss of Death
Kiss of Revenge

Sweet Seasons

The Summer of Cotton Candy
The Fall of Candy Corn
The Winter of Candy Canes
The Spring of Candy Apples

Robin Hood Demon's Bane (with James R. Tuck)

Mark of the Black Arrow

Tex Ravencroft Adventures (with Dr. Scott C. Viguié)

The Tears of Poseidon
The Brotherhood of Lies

THY ROD AND THY STAFF

Psalm 23 Mysteries

By Debbie Viguié

Published by Big Pink Bow

Thy Rod and Thy Staff

ISBN-13: 978-0-9906971-4-5

Published by Big Pink Bow

www.bigpinkbow.com

Dedicated to my Bible Study Group. You are the craziest, most awesome people and I love you all.

Thank you to everyone who helped make this book a reality, particularly Barbara Reynolds, Rick Reynolds, Rita De La Torre, and Calliope Collacott. Thank you to Diane Woodall who has been a Godsend the last several months and has helped keep me sane. A great big thank you to Serena Webb, an awesome fan and winner of my last year's Halloween contest to have a character named after her.

1

Jeremiah Silverman had always liked Tuesdays. Compared to the rest of the week they seemed quiet and he was usually able to get a lot of work done. Rarely did he have any meetings scheduled on Tuesdays, and it was the one day of the week where the fewest people dropped by the synagogue office unannounced. It was also the day during the week when he and Cindy were most likely to go to lunch together.

There was no lunch scheduled for that day, though, and he found that he was out of sorts as he parked in the synagogue parking lot. As he got out of his car he glanced over into the church's parking lot and realized he was looking for Cindy's car.

It wasn't there. He didn't know why he'd been looking in the first place. It hadn't been there the day before either. A now familiar twinge of uneasiness crept through him. He didn't like it when he couldn't keep his eyes on her all the time. The last couple of weeks had only intensified things, too. After all, since they had become engaged he felt like he had even more to lose.

"She's just at jury duty," he said out loud, hoping to calm himself down. It didn't work, and he turned and headed toward the office with a sigh.

When he walked into the main office his secretary, Marie, looked up from a stack of papers on her desk. Her mouth set into a hard, thin line and she glared daggers at him. It had been the same every day since Valentine's Day when he had proposed to Cindy, making their private relationship suddenly very public.

"Morning, Marie," he said, forcing a smile onto his face.

She didn't say anything, just continued to glare. He walked to his office, slower than he normally would have, to let her know that her disapproval didn't bother him. His hand was on the door to his office when she spoke up.

"I need to go over some of the Purim arrangements with you."

He turned back, careful to keep his smile in place. "Alright."

She rolled her eyes as she folded her arms over her chest, a defensive reaction. "The carnival games and the bounce houses are going to arrive the night before for set-up."

"Excellent."

"We still need at least eight more volunteers to help run things."

"I'll see what I can do on Saturday to find some."

"Good luck with that," she said, scowling.

He didn't know if she was referring to the usual difficulties with getting enough volunteers to work an event or if there was something more going on. He decided not to ask, at least, not at the moment. "What else?"

"Have you talked to the Gentile pastor about using their parking lot during the event?"

Jeremiah barely contained what he wanted to say. Marie was the only person he knew who used that word. The way she had spit it out he could tell she was even more disgusted by the Gentiles than usual. He assumed that was because of Cindy.

“I’ll talk to him today,” Jeremiah said, not anticipating a problem. The church next door and the synagogue had always had a friendly arrangement whereby each used the other’s parking lot when needed. The two were separated only by a very short hedge that had paths cut through it. There shouldn’t be too much of a problem using the church’s parking lot for the Purim festival, particularly since it would be a weekday event.

“Good.”

“Is there anything else?” he asked.

She shook her head.

He glanced at his office door but decided to go talk to the pastor first and get it out of the way. “I’ll be back in a couple of minutes,” he said as he left.

As he crossed over to the church he couldn’t help but wonder if Marie would ever accept Cindy. He was beginning to doubt it. Why he should expect different he didn’t know. There was only so long he could ignore her disapproval and her scathing looks, though, before he snapped at her. That was something he didn’t want to do.

He was close to the church offices when he saw Geanie exit the main office. She glanced at him in surprise. “Cindy’s not here,” she said as he approached.

“I know, I’m here to talk to Pastor Ben,” he said smiling.

“I just saw him head into the sanctuary,” she said.

“Thanks.”

He altered course and headed for the sanctuary. That was where he and Cindy had first met when she’d found the dead body and he’d heard her screaming. He had seen her in the church parking lot before that and noticed how attractive she was, but he had never known her name until that day.

He shook his head in amazement at the events that had transpired that had thrown them together, and then the events that had kept them together. G-d had certainly had a plan for the two of them, even when he himself hadn't seen it.

The lights were on in the sanctuary and he could see Ben sitting in the pew up front. Jeremiah hesitated for a moment, but it didn't look like the man was praying. He approached slowly, making just enough noise to alert the pastor to his presence but not enough to disturb him if he was praying.

When Jeremiah was just a couple of feet away the man turned and looked at him. He frowned.

"Rabbi, what are you doing here?"

"I came to talk to you about next week's Purim celebration," Jeremiah said.

"Have a seat," Ben said, sliding down the pew a couple of feet to make room.

"Thanks."

"Purim, that commemorates Esther saving her people, right?"

"Yes. It's one of our more festive celebrations, basically a chance to throw a great party," Jeremiah said with a smile as he took the offered seat.

"So, why did you want to talk?" Ben asked.

"We're going to need to borrow your parking lot. We're going to be using part of ours for the event and we always have a lot more people show up for Purim than we expect."

"Sure. Double check the master calendar with Cindy, but I'm pretty sure we don't have anything going on next week that would cause a problem."

"Great, thank you."

Jeremiah sat for a couple seconds more and then started to get up.

"Rabbi?"

"Yes, Pastor?" he asked, sitting back down.

"Esther had to hide her religion from the king, her husband, until the lives of her people were threatened."

"Yes, that's true," Jeremiah said, wondering where Ben was going with his statement.

"Are you expecting Cindy to hide her religion?"

"Excuse me?" he asked, startled.

"You heard me. You're a rabbi. Are you expecting her to convert or will you just be satisfied with her hiding that aspect of her life, suppressing it?"

"Cindy is a wonderful woman of faith. That's one of the things that's most attractive about her," Jeremiah said, feeling fire creeping along his veins. "I would never want her to suppress her beliefs or stop practicing her religion."

"And yet that's what will happen. The husband is the head of the household and even if you're tolerant now, when that household expands to include children you're going to want them raised Jewish, not Christian. And Cindy will give in."

Jeremiah stood. "I don't think you really understand her or respect her. Or me," he said. Anger was pouring through him now and he realized he should leave before he said or did something he would regret later.

"There's not much to understand. She's a woman in love and they aren't known for making the wisest decisions," Ben said, staring up at him. "Frankly I am surprised a bit at you, though. You're a rabbi, a leader, expected to set an example. I can't imagine your congregation will be all too thrilled with you marrying outside the faith. Which just leads me to believe that deep down you think it's not going to be an issue. Hence my concern for Cindy's spiritual well-being."

Jeremiah took a deep breath. "Thank you for your concern, but it's really not your concern."

"Oh, but it is," Ben said, standing up. "I'm her pastor. And she works for the church so she has to set an example as well. The two of you aren't isolated, you are the head of the synagogue and she's the church secretary which means hundreds of people think they're her boss and that what she does matters. Both of you are obligated to set good examples, to live upright and moral lives. You have responsibilities to others. You're not living your lives in a vacuum. Your actions will have consequences, ripples that will go on forever impacting thousands of people. You can't afford to be blind to that. None of us can. I've already had people come up to me, worried that Cindy is marrying outside the faith. And they have a right to be worried, not just for her but also for the example she's setting for their children or grandchildren."

Jeremiah clenched his hands into fists at his side. Ben had just very subtly threatened Cindy's job. The urge to tear him apart limb by limb was nearly overwhelming. Once upon a time he would probably have been able to suppress the emotion, but Cindy had broken through his barriers, gotten him to love, to feel, and as a result all his emotions were nearer the surface, harder to control than they once had been.

Which was why he couldn't afford to stand there a second longer. If he did, it would be too easy to hit the pastor. And with his background, one act of violence could easily escalate depending on the other man's response.

Jeremiah turned and walked away, not trusting himself to say even a single word. The worst part was that Ben had touched on some of the things Jeremiah himself had worried about, namely acceptance by those around them. Or, rather, lack thereof.

He wished he could call Cindy. Just hearing her voice was oftentimes enough to calm him down. He'd just have to wait, though, and pray that he could get the fire he felt inside under control before he took his frustration out on someone who didn't deserve it.

~

Detective Mark Walters was on edge. He had been for the last couple of days, ever since Jason Todd had arrived in town to be tried for murder. The man was a tech guy from Silicon Valley up in the northern part of the state. He was accused of killing his wife, and the media up there had so sensationalized the case that finding an untainted jury pool had proven impossible. So here he was, in Pine Springs, and he had brought hell with him.

Hell, in this particular instance, was a sea of picketers and press who had come from as far as three states away. Currently they were all stretched out around the courthouse and the Pine Springs police department had all hands on deck for as long as the craziness was going to last. Instead of taking the weekend off to spend with Traci and the twins like he'd hoped, Mark had instead worked a twelve hour shift each day. That had been followed up by a fourteen hour shift on Monday. He wasn't holding out any hope that this day would end any better.

What made it worse was that they'd ended up with less time to prepare for the onslaught than they'd been told they'd have. Apparently that bit of misinformation had been disseminated in an attempt to throw the picketers and press off the scent. Turned out, though, that the only ones fooled and caught unaware by the fake timeline were the police.

"I can't wait until they declare him guilty and this whole thing goes away," Mark growled.

"You think he did it?" Liam, his partner, asked.

"Yeah, then again, he didn't do much to make himself look innocent."

"People grieve in different ways."

"And some not at all. In my opinion he's one of them."

"Which might make him guilty of not caring, but it doesn't make him guilty of murder," Liam protested.

"He sure didn't do much to help identify someone else as the killer."

"You're thinking like a cop and not a civilian," Liam said with a shake of his head.

Mark almost responded with a comment that Cindy or Jeremiah certainly would have helped track down the other's killer, but realized that wasn't his best argument. Given his background Jeremiah couldn't exactly be called a civilian and Cindy just seemed to be a special case all the way around.

The truth was, concern for her was just making this whole mess more worrisome for him. He knew he was probably being paranoid, but Cindy always seemed to manage to find trouble and as far as he was concerned the Jason Todd trial was nothing but.

"I heard the Vegas casinos are taking bets on the outcome of the trial," Liam said. "If you're so certain he's guilty maybe you should make a little wager."

"You're not serious."

"Afraid so. I heard they were taking bets on innocent versus guilty and on what sentencing will be if he is found guilty."

"It's disgusting what people will decide to treat like a spectator sport," Mark said glumly.

He sighed, wishing for a moment that he was religious so that he could at least pray. If he could he'd be praying that his friend didn't get picked to be on the jury for the trial.

~

Cindy had been sitting for a day and a half in a large room at the courthouse with a bunch of other people, most of whom wanted to be out of there just as much as she did. She had found the day before that she was too anxious to read the book she'd brought. She really had no desire to be on a jury and if the rumors running around the room were true she really didn't want to be on this one in particular.

Today instead of the book she'd brought with her a stack of bridal magazines that Geanie had bought her the day after she and Jeremiah had become engaged. Cindy felt herself flushing just at the memory as she glanced down at the ring on her finger. She'd stared at the heart-shaped diamond a thousand times in the last few days and she knew she'd never get sick of it.

"It's beautiful," the woman beside her said suddenly.

Cindy jumped slightly, startled. "Thanks," she said, feeling herself flush even more.

The woman had auburn hair that curled at the edges, pretty features, and some freckles on her cheeks. She was staring at Cindy's ring admiringly. "I've never seen a heart-shaped diamond. The man who gave that to you must be pretty special."

"He is," Cindy said, unable to stop the smile that spread across her face.

"When's the wedding?"

"I don't know yet. We just got engaged."

"Congratulations. I've always thought December weddings were nice."

Cindy felt her heart skip a beat. She'd always thought so, too. "I don't know. I don't think I can get everything ready by December. We're trying not to rush. Besides, that's one of the busiest times of year for both of us," she said, giving voice to her own misgivings.

"So, plan for the December after next."

Cindy could feel a growing excitement deep inside. A December wedding would be magical.

"So, what do you do that December is so busy?"

"He's a rabbi and I'm a church secretary."

The other woman's chocolate brown eyes widened slightly. "Wow, I bet you are busy. Are you the secretary at his church or synagogue I guess I should say?"

"Oh no. I'm a secretary at First Shepherd."

"So, you're Christian, not Jewish?"

Cindy nodded her head.

"Your wedding's going to be complicated."

Cindy grimaced slightly at the reminder.

"Oh, I'm so sorry, I didn't mean to say that or make you feel bad."

"No, it's okay. You're not wrong."

"I'm Serena, by the way. Serena Webb."

"Cindy Preston," Cindy said, shaking the other woman's hand.

"Nice to meet you," Serena said with a smile that lit up her face. "Actually, it's really nice to meet you. I haven't had a chance to actually get acquainted with anyone since I moved here."

"You're new to the area?"

"Yes, moved about six weeks ago. I could hardly believe it when I got the jury summons."

"Welcome to Pine Springs," Cindy said with a little laugh. "Yeah, jury duty isn't exactly the best welcome party. So, what brought you here?"

Serena seemed to hesitate for a moment before finally saying, "I needed a change and I guess I moved here looking for roots or something. I think my mom grew up somewhere around here."

"Where does she live now?"

Serena winced and Cindy reached out and touched her arm. "I'm sorry," she murmured.

"It's okay, it was a long time ago. I never really knew her. I lived with my aunt growing up. She passed away a couple of months ago, though." Serena took a deep breath. "So, I decided to get the heck out of town and try something new for a while."

"That's brave of you," Cindy said.

Serena just shrugged. "You know, I've been so busy the last few weeks I haven't even had a chance to look for a church. I think I've driven by First Shepherd a couple of times. Would you recommend it?"

"I would," Cindy said.

"Is there a choir? I like to sing."

"We have a great choir. Our whole arts and music department is pretty spectacular. Sabrina, the co-director for the choir, is always looking for new members, too."

"That sounds nice."

"You should give the church a try. Some great people go there."

"I have a feeling some great people work there, too," Serena said teasingly.

Before Cindy could respond, the speakers in the room crackled to life. "Would jurors 104 to 139 please report to the desk. Jurors 104 to 139 to the front desk please."

Cindy double checked her summons notice even though she knew she was 127. After confirming, she shoved the bridal magazines back into her bag and rose. "Let's hope they're sending me home," she said.

"Good luck," Serena said.

"Thanks."

She walked to the front of the room to the desk where she had initially checked in. She glanced around at the others gathering there, too, and saw a mixture of hope and dread on the faces around her. She was pretty sure they all just wanted to go home. There was one, though, who stood out because he had a look of eager excitement on his face. He looked like he was in his late twenties and was clutching a massive backpack that looked heavy. In a sea full of tired, bored people who wanted to be somewhere else he stood out.

They all stood there for about five minutes, waiting to hear their fate. The woman behind the counter was on the phone, but Cindy wasn't close enough to make out what she was saying. At last the woman hung up the phone, typed something on her computer keyboard, then stood up as a man in a uniform came in the door.

"Alright, jurors 104 to 139 please follow the bailiff," the woman said, indicating the man.

"Stay together," the man instructed before opening the door and leading the way out.

Cindy's heart sank. They weren't being sent home, they were being sent to the next round of jury selection.

2

Cindy and the others followed the bailiff and they soon found themselves inside a courtroom. The walls were all rich, dark wood and the whole room had an air of authority and intimidation to it. She guessed that was the point. As they took their seats, Cindy couldn't help but stare at the people up front. A judge and two people she assumed were attorneys were speaking together and looking at sheets of paper.

"I can't be here, it's my turn to pick up my kid at school," a guy in his thirties, wearing a blue work shirt with the sleeves rolled up and khaki pants, muttered next to her.

"Just tell them you know how to spot a guilty person just like that," the woman on the other side of him whispered, ending with a snap of her fingers.

He chuckled. "You think that would actually work?"

"Couldn't hurt," she said.

"My cousin got out of jury duty that way," a guy in the row behind them chimed in.

Cindy bit her lip to keep from smiling. For a brief moment she imagined everyone up and down the line saying the same thing. Somehow she had a feeling that the men up front wouldn't buy it. After all, they had to realize that the majority of the people in the room didn't want to be there, and they'd probably heard every excuse there was.

Finally the men up at the front of the room seemed to finish whatever discussion they were having and they turned their attention on the prospective jurors.

The judge cleared his throat and the murmuring around her ceased instantly as all eyes turned to him. "Ladies and gentlemen, we are going to be asking you several questions. We ask that you answer as truthfully as possible as this will make the entire process smoother for everyone. The case that we are going to be trying could last up to two weeks. Employers are required to give you the time off to serve. However, the state of California does not compel them to pay you for the time that you will be here. Some employers do and some don't."

They then went up and down the line asking each person if they would be compensated by their employer for the time they spent serving. Several people took the opportunity to explain in detail how serving would be a hardship upon them and their families. When it came to her she answered truthfully that the church did pay for time spent in jury duty.

Once they were finished with that the judge continued. "This trial will be a murder trial. Raise your hand if you've known anyone who was murdered or have known anyone who was a murderer."

Faces flashed through Cindy's mind as she raised her hand. Unfortunately thanks to the events of the last few years she knew both. She was surprised to see a number of other hands go up until she stopped and thought about the sheer number of fatalities in Pine Springs over the last couple of years. The Passion Week Killer had claimed almost two dozen citizens of the town, any of whom could have been friends of some of the people around her. More faces came to her. The women who'd been killed in the explosion at the bridal shop right before Geanie and Joseph's wedding. It was possible they'd sold dresses to one of the three other women in the room who had their hands in the air.

And then there was the other side of things. How many people there had eaten at O'Connell's pub until its owner, Chris, was arrested along with his brother and one of their friends for murder? If it hadn't been for years of practice throwing darts at a picture of her brother she would have become another one of their victims.

Cindy shivered, the interconnectedness of it all suddenly hitting her in a big way.

Suddenly she realized that one of the attorneys had asked her a question.

"I'm sorry, what did you say?" she asked a little sheepishly.

"In our legal system people are innocent until proven guilty. Since you've had experience either knowing a murderer or their victim do you think you could be objective while listening to the evidence or would your emotions get in the way?"

"I would hope I could be objective. I've also had friends who were falsely accused so I appreciate that people are innocent until proven guilty. I think it would depend honestly on the facts at hand as to whether or not my emotions would interfere, though."

Both attorneys nodded their heads and she couldn't tell if what she had said helped ensure that she would get out of jury duty or be stuck with it. They asked a similar question of everyone who had raised a hand.

Cindy would have thought that would be the end of it, but there were still several more rounds of questions where it was clear both attorneys were trying to get a feel for how open-minded or how easily persuaded each of the potential jurors was. There were also a couple of questions about living arrangements, if anyone was the sole caregiver for a child or an elderly parent. For her part she answered everything as honestly as she could.

At last they excused them to go to lunch, giving them forty-five minutes. Cindy made her way to the cafeteria in the building since she didn't have time to really go anywhere else. She grabbed an egg salad sandwich and a Coca Cola and found a table.

A minute later one of the men who had been in the room with her stepped over with his own sandwich. "Mind if I join you?" he asked.

"Not at all," she said, moving her drink to give him more room on the table.

He sat down across from her.

"It's fascinating, you know?" he said.

"What?"

"The whole process. I mean, can you imagine getting on a murder trial?"

"I'm trying not to," Cindy admitted.

"I think it's so interesting, just to see the whole process. You know, I keep wondering if we're being considered for the Jason Todd trial. Wouldn't that be crazy?"

"The guy from northern California? I wouldn't want to be a part of that," Cindy said. As much as she disliked following news even she had heard about that case. The jurors would likely come in for a huge amount of scrutiny from the press which was exactly what she didn't need.

"I'm Tanner, by the way," the guy said, holding out his hand.

"Cindy," she said, shaking his hand and noticing how firm his grip was.

They continued to make small talk for a couple of minutes and then Cindy excused herself to the restroom to freshen up. When it was time, she made her way back to the bailiff as she had been instructed. Tanner was already there, hands in pockets and a small smile on his face.

The others arrived shortly after, and the bailiff sent half of them back to the jury room. The other half, including Cindy, Tanner, and the guy who had been sitting next to her in the blue work shirt followed him back into the courtroom.

Already inside the courtroom were a few other people Cindy had seen in the jury room early that morning who had been called before she had. Her stomach tightened slightly as she realized she must be part of the final pool that they were going to be selecting from. There were about two dozen of them in all.

"We have just a couple more questions for all of you," the one attorney said. "Raise your hand if you've heard anything in the news or anywhere else about Jason Todd."

Cindy felt her stomach twist slightly. Tanner had been right to guess which trial they were being considered for. All but three hands went into the air, including hers. The guy in the blue work shirt kept his hand down and shook his head slowly. A woman in her sixties who was sitting two seats away also kept her hand down. She blinked in surprise when she realized that the third person who didn't raise a hand was Tanner.

Why would he lie? She knew for a fact that he knew who Jason Todd was. He had seemed so eager to be on the jury for that trial. Was that why he was lying now and not raising his hand? She debated about whether she should say something, but it would just be her word against his.

A young woman who looked like she was probably still in college was the first one on the end of Cindy's row. The attorney walked up to stand in front of her. "How much have you heard about the case?"

"I just know that he was a suspect in his wife's murder. I saw a couple things as newspaper headlines. I'm a full time student, and I don't watch much television, and my computer is ancient, and it's too hard to do anything on it except write my term papers."

"What are you studying in school?"

"I'm studying to be a teacher."

"Do you believe that you could put aside what you've heard and you could be objective, not form an opinion one way or another before hearing all the facts of the case?"

"I think so," she said.

He nodded and then moved on to the next person, asking them similar questions. At last he made it to Cindy.

"How much have you heard?" he asked.

"Honestly, I've heard the name. I've heard that he was accused of killing his wife, although from what I understand her body is still missing, at least, that's what I heard."

"Is that all?"

"Yes. I try to avoid the news as much as I can. It's usually too depressing."

"Are you capable of being objective, Miss Preston?"

Cindy was surprised. She was the only one he had called by name. She nodded slowly.

"Thank you, Miss Preston."

The other attorney stepped forward suddenly. "Miss Preston, it is well known that you have had a hand in helping the police capture a number of criminals, including murderers. Are you sure that your own experience and background will enable you to not jump to conclusions?"

That was why they called her by name, they knew who she was. Cindy took a deep breath. "What I've learned from that experience is that things are complicated, and often it looks like someone might be guilty, but without all the facts you can't really say that they are for sure."

Everyone was looking at her intently, even her fellow juror candidates and she felt intensely uncomfortable. There was a long moment of silence before the first attorney turned and began questioning the next person.

Half an hour later they wrapped up their questions. Then the two attorneys conferred with the judge, speaking quietly and shuffling some papers. Around her people fidgeted uncomfortably. At last they were done and they called the bailiff up. They handed him a piece of paper and he approached Cindy and the others. He called off a list of numbers and then said, "Come with me."

Cindy was not on the list and she watched as those who were got up and followed the bailiff out of the room. After the door had closed behind them the judge addressed those who remained.

"Ladies and gentlemen. You have been selected to be the jury with jurors 105 and 116 serving as the designated alternates for the trial which will begin tomorrow. As this case has attracted a lot of media attention, and we do not wish to expose you to any further outside information or harassment by the press, this jury will be sequestered. Each of you will be escorted to your home by a police officer where you will pack clothes and toiletries enough for two weeks. You'll also have an opportunity to make any other arrangements you need to. Tonight at nine the police officer assigned to you will escort you to the hotel where you will be staying during the trial."

Murmurs of outrage rose around her and Cindy just stared. She couldn't believe that not only had she ended up on the jury but that she was also going to be sequestered. She glanced around at her fellow jurors. Only Tanner was smiling.

~

Mark's phone rang on the seat next to him. The crowds around the courthouse that they were once again circling were so heavy and unpredictable that he needed both hands on the steering wheel. "Grab that for me," he told Liam.

Liam answered and a minute later hung up. "The good news is we can leave this insanity, at least for a few minutes."

"That is good news," Mark said as he barely managed to swerve around a man who careened out into the street. "What's the bad news?"

"Bad news is it's probably a wild goose chase and we'll be right back here in an hour."

"I'll take it. An hour away is better than nothing. Where are we headed?"

"Fourth and Pine. A lady who owns a tea shop reported a murder on Sunday."

"Two days ago? Why didn't we go out there Sunday?" Mark asked.

"A patrol car was dispatched but supposedly couldn't find anything. Apparently she is insisting on speaking to detectives now."

"I'm happy to talk to her all day if it means getting out of patrol duty," Mark said.

Ten minutes later they were parking outside of Tea Thyme, a quaint little shop that sported a wide variety of teapots and teacups in its windows. A minute later they were inside and being greeted by a petite, pretty red-haired woman.

"I'm Rebecca Thyme," she said, extending her hand.

"As in Tea Thyme," Liam said, a grin on his face as he shook her hand.

"Exactly."

"I'm Mark and this is my partner, Liam," Mark said when it was his turn to shake, noting that his partner had managed to forget the introductions.

"Thank you for coming," Rebecca said.

"It's no problem," Liam said, smiling even more broadly.

"We understand you reported a murder Sunday evening," Mark said.

"Yes. It was just after eight o'clock. I had worked late to get ready for a private function on Monday. I locked up and started walking home. I only live about a mile away and it always seems like a waste to drive such a short distance so most days I walk. I was passing by an alley a couple blocks from here when I heard a scuffling sound. It was dark, but there was a street lamp close by and I could make out two men struggling. I saw the glint of light off a knife and then the man who was holding it stabbed the other one who fell. I ran back to my shop and I dialed 911 and reported it."

"Then what happened?" Mark asked.

"Two patrolmen came. They said they checked the alley but found no signs of a body. I walked them over there, they took a couple of notes, and then said someone would be in contact with me. I gave up waiting and finally called the police station only to be informed that there was no active investigation. You can imagine my horror."

"Is it possible you misinterpreted what you saw? It was dark, after all," Mark said.

"It was, but I have excellent vision and I know what I saw."

"Can you show us the spot?"

She nodded and led them outside. She put the Closed sign in the window and locked the door before setting out at a brisk walk up the street. Two blocks later she turned into an alley that ran between a dry cleaners and a vacant building. She stopped about two-thirds of the way down the alley.

"Here is where they were, just a couple of feet from that dumpster," she said, pointing to the large trash receptacle that was against the wall of the vacant building.

Mark and Liam both squatted down to take a closer look at the ground. There were no tell-tale signs of blood. They stood and walked the length of the alley, opening the two dumpsters that were there. Mark shook his head slowly, realizing there was nothing to see.

They walked back to Rebecca who was watching them intently, arms folded across her chest. “Let me guess, you don’t see anything,” she said, a touch of sarcasm in her voice.

“No, ma’am,” Liam said.

“Are you sure the man who was stabbed was dead? It’s possible he was just injured and he ran off,” Mark said.

“He died. I know that for a fact,” she said.

“How?” Mark asked. “From what you’ve told us you ran right back to your shop and didn’t have an opportunity to examine the body.”

“I didn’t need to. You ever hear the sound a dying man makes when he is choking on his own blood?”

“Yes,” Mark said, surprised at the question.

“Then you’ll understand when I tell you he was a dead man, even if I left before he was completely gone.”

“And how is it a tea shop owner comes to be familiar with that sound?” Mark couldn’t stop himself from asking.

Rebecca lifted a shapely eyebrow. “I served in the army. Did two tours in Afghanistan. I know that sound all too well.”

“Ah, understood,” Mark said. He wouldn’t have pegged her as former military. It just went to show that people were always full of surprises.

“Why did you go all the way back to the shop to call? Why not just get out of sight and call on your smart phone?” Liam asked.

“Because I’m a luddite. I don’t have a portable phone. I believe in a simpler way of life, before technology took over and destroyed our ability to relate to people in a normal way.”

Mark couldn't help but wonder if her experiences in the army and whatever trauma she might be suffering as a result had led to her desire for a simpler life.

"I've never been overly fond of smart phones myself," Liam said. "Feels like you're wearing a leash everywhere you go."

"Exactly," she said, suddenly smiling.

Mark bit his tongue before he could say that he'd never heard Liam criticize cell phones before. It was quickly becoming evident that his partner was more than a little taken with Rebecca.

"Did you get a good look at either man's face?" Mark asked.

"Unfortunately, no. I can tell you that the victim's hair was light, blond most likely. I didn't get a good look at his face, though. His attacker was wearing a hoodie so I couldn't even tell that much about him."

Mark knew why the responding officers had written off Rebecca and her story. With no physical evidence at the scene and her inability to describe either man there was nowhere to go, no proof that a crime had been committed and no way to even try and follow up.

"You believe me, right?" she suddenly asked.

"We absolutely believe you," Liam said before Mark could answer.

"Good, so what do you do next?" she asked.

Mark sighed. "We'll get a forensics team down here to go over everything. Maybe they can find some trace blood evidence or something."

It was a long shot, but she seemed certain and if she had witnessed a murder it was their responsibility to see the killer brought to justice. He was about to call it in when something caught his eye a few feet away. He walked over. It was a corner of a piece of paper that had been torn. There could be any number of such bits of trash in the alley, but this one didn't look like it had been out in the elements too long. It was very white except for a stain at the edge that was reddish brown.

Blood.

3

Jeremiah realized rationally that he shouldn't be as upset as he was. As he sat on Cindy's porch and waited for her to arrive with her police escort he took several deep breaths. It wasn't like she was going to be going far. She was just going to be in a hotel a couple miles away for the next two weeks. She would be close and safe, even if he couldn't see her.

She'd called him from the courthouse restroom to let him know what was going on. He didn't like it. He didn't like that she was going to be involved in such a high profile trial or that he wasn't going to be able to see her. It wasn't fair. They were barely engaged and he already hated every moment that they were apart.

He was also debating about whether or not he should tell her that the pastor at First Shepherd was against their relationship. On the one hand he might have already made his feelings on the subject known to her. If he hadn't, though, speaking up now could keep her from getting blindsided one day at work. He had just about decided to wait to tell her until after the trial. There was no use giving her something to stew over for the next couple of weeks when there was no chance that she would run into the man during that time. She'd have enough to worry about with the sequester.

Cindy's car finally turned onto the street, followed closely by a police car, and he got to his feet. Both cars pulled into the driveway and the drivers were out of the cars seconds later.

"Thanks for escorting me home. Can you pick me up in about three hours?" Cindy asked the officer.

He shook his head. "Sorry, ma'am, for your safety I'm to stay with you until you're packed and ready to go to the hotel."

Jeremiah's fists clenched at his side. So much for any shot at privacy. "I think I can guarantee her safety," he said.

Cindy sighed. "I think he's also here to make sure I don't spend the next two hours on the internet learning everything I can about Jason Todd."

The officer grimaced slightly, but didn't say anything.

"Okay, let's get this over with," Cindy said, leading the way to the front door.

Inside she waved the officer to a seat in the living room and Jeremiah followed her back to her bedroom. She grabbed a suitcase from her closet and threw it on the bed with a tired sigh.

"This is so not what I had planned for the next two weeks," she said.

Jeremiah wrapped an arm around her waist and spun her toward him. "Me either," he said before bending to kiss her.

When they finally broke apart Cindy moved to her closet and started grabbing clothes to toss into her suitcase. Jeremiah sat on the edge of her bed, feeling worse than useless.

"I don't like this," he said.

"Neither do I."

"What if something happens?"

She turned and looked at him. "What do you mean?"

He sighed. "In case you haven't noticed, things rarely go well when we're apart."

She stared at him for several seconds and then burst out laughing.

"What?" he asked.

"Things don't always go well even when we are together," she said.

He wished he found it as amusing as she did. She wasn't wrong, though. Trouble had a way of finding them.

"This isn't like Hawaii or Las Vegas. I'm going to be here, in town, surrounded by police and lawyers and bailiffs and a whole bunch of other people who are going to be in the same boat with me. I'm going to be miserable and I'm going to go crazy missing you, but I think I'll be safe enough," she said with a smile.

Everything she said made sense. He just wished he could overcome his own trepidation. A lifetime of paranoia, with good reason, and too many close calls involving her kept him from being able to take comfort in what she was saying.

"Where are you staying?" he asked.

"They won't tell me. I just know it's a hotel."

"I'll find you."

She laid a hand on his arm. "I'm sure Mark will tell you, so you don't need to follow us or anything."

Jeremiah smiled for her sake. "Of course Mark will tell me. He's not stupid."

She leaned down and gave him a quick kiss. “And I have full faith in your ability to keep an eye on me with no one knowing.”

He wished he had access to a fraction of the tools he used to use in his old line of work. There was no help for that, though, and he’d have to make do with what he had.

~

The forensics team had swept the alley and found evidence of blood. While there were a number of reasons why blood might be present on the asphalt, the amount of it that was found where their witness said the stabbing had taken place was enough for Mark to classify it as a homicide investigation. It was possible that his judgment was tainted by the fact that he’d rather work an investigation than work on crowd control at the courthouse. Liam, though, didn’t bat an eye. Then again his judgment was clearly being affected by his desire to spend more time talking to Rebecca.

They walked back to her tea shop where she was waiting.

“Did they find anything?” she asked as she opened the door for them.

“Trace evidence of blood, quite a lot of it, right where you indicated the man was stabbed,” Liam said.

She nodded and Mark could detect a hint of relief in her eyes. Someone believed her and even though she had witnessed something horrific there was comfort in not feeling alone in her knowledge.

“So, what happens next?” Rebecca asked as she sat down at one of the tables.

Mark and Liam took seats as well. The table was set with a tea pot and delicate cups decorated with silver blue roses. Traci would love it. Maybe he should bring her sometime.

"Next we ask you a bunch of questions trying to figure out everything we can about what happened," Liam said.

He didn't usually take lead when talking to witnesses, at least, not so aggressively. Mark hid a smile by turning his head to glance around at the rest of the tea shop. The place was quaint and very neat and precise. Everything seemed to have a place and was displayed just so. Even the tables were that way with every utensil placed exactly. He suspected that Rebecca was a woman who liked order in her life, and a large amount of control. Whether she had always been that way or it was a reaction to her time in the military he didn't know.

He turned back to the table he was at and tried a small experiment. He touched the tea pot, as though admiring it, and nudged it slightly out of the center of the table before letting go. Rebecca glanced down and he could see her hand twitch once, twice, then she reached out and reset the tea pot.

Most people who reported witnessing a crime wouldn't bother to call back and follow up. Most would want to put the whole business behind them and would be happy to let others take care of the problem. Chaos had entered Rebecca's carefully ordered world, though, and she wasn't the type that could let that go without resolution.

He just hoped they could get some for her.

"You said the victim had light hair, probably blond," Mark said, pulling out his notepad.

"That's correct."

"About how tall was he?"

"I'd say around five foot ten. The man who attacked him was about two inches taller."

"What kind of build?"

"Average for both although the taller man was slightly thinner."

"You said the attacker was wearing a hoodie," Liam said.

"Yes, a black one and black pants as well."

"Where did he pull the knife from?" Mark asked.

"The back of his waistband. I'm not sure, but I think he had a sheath for it there."

"Could you see anything distinctive about the knife?" Mark asked.

"No, the blade was about six inches, but the handle was completely covered by his hand."

"Okay, what about the victim? What kind of clothes was he wearing?"

"It looked like he was wearing jeans and a darker colored shirt, long sleeves."

"T-shirt, button down, collar, no collar?"

She shook her head. "It was a little loose on him, but I don't know what kind of shirt."

"Okay, that's okay," Mark said biting down his own frustration. "You said you heard a scuffling sound, they were already wrestling with each other when you first saw them?"

"Yes."

"But the attacker pulled out the knife after you first saw them?"

"Just after, he was reaching for it when I first laid eyes on them."

"Did either of them say anything?" Liam asked. "Either before you saw them or after?"

"No, I'm sorry. They just made grunting sounds, like two people fighting really hard."

"Was either of them holding something like a piece of paper?" Mark asked, thinking of the blood soaked scrap he had found.

She paused, her brow wrinkling as she thought. Then slowly she shook her head. "I don't know. I can't be sure. Not the killer, he had the knife in his right hand and he had the guy's shirt balled up in his other fist. I couldn't see the victim's right hand so I don't know if he was holding something in it or not."

"Did either man notice you?" Liam asked, concern heavy in his voice.

"No, I'm sure they didn't. They were too focused on each other."

"That's good," Liam said.

"In your estimation, how much time passed between the stabbing and the officers arriving at the alley?" Mark asked.

"Probably ten minutes. No more than fifteen."

Which meant the killer had gotten rid of the body, cleaned up the blood that would have pooled on the ground, and been nowhere around by the time the police got there. He had moved fast. He hadn't bothered to try and remove the trace evidence of blood, though, which meant he either knew he didn't have time or he didn't think he needed to.

"Were there any cars parked in the alley or close by that you can recall?" Mark asked.

Rebecca paused again, clearly thinking. Finally she answered. "I believe I walked by a pickup truck before I got to the alley. When I went back with the officers there weren't any cars, though, except theirs."

"Can you describe the truck? Color, make?" Mark asked hopefully.

She shook her head. "I wasn't paying attention, to be honest. The only reason I even remember seeing it in the first place was that it was parked next to a fire hydrant and I thought to myself that someone was going to end up with a ticket."

Mark closed his notebook, unable to contain a sigh of frustration.

"I'm sorry I'm not more help," she said, wrinkling up her nose.

"No, you've done great," Liam hastened to assure her.

"What now?" she asked.

"Now, we hope that somebody reports a missing person. Until then we don't have anything to really go on," Mark admitted. "If you can think of any other detail, no matter how slight, please don't hesitate to call us."

Before he could hand her a card Liam was already putting one in her hand. "Call day or night, for anything," his partner said earnestly. "Even if you just need to talk."

"Thank you," she said, staring into his eyes.

The two of them stood there, just staring intently at each other.

Mark cleared his throat. "Okay, we'll be in touch." He tapped Liam on the shoulder. "Let's go partner."

"I need to close up for the evening anyway," Rebecca said. "Tea is an afternoon activity. After five no one really cares, but I usually stay open until six in case any of my customers want to pick up some tea to take home after work. I sell several specialty varieties."

"Really? Maybe I should get some," Liam said.

Mark fought the urge to roll his eyes as he realized he was going to practically have to carry Liam out of there.

"I'd be happy to make some recommendations, especially if you're new to tea drinking," Rebecca said.

"I love tea," Liam said.

Mark realized he didn't know if that was true or not. After a year and a half as partners he should know stuff like that. He couldn't even remember at the moment how Liam took his coffee. The other man always made the coffee runs.

Mark hunched his shoulders, feeling suddenly bad. He had known what Paul liked to drink and he would never have touched tea, calling it the drink of the idle rich. It had been an ironic statement given that his family fell into that category. Well, his fake family at any rate.

There was still so much about Paul that he didn't know and the mysteries just kept piling up. He still hadn't been able to translate the coded letter Paul's widow had given him or the coded files Paul's attorney had kept in a secret safe in his house. He needed to find out what they said, and soon. Everything was in chaos right now, though, and finding time was difficult.

He glanced again at Liam. Mark had known all the daily likes and foibles of his old partner but hadn't known what was really important, the secrets the man was hiding from him. With a start he realized that he didn't know as much about Liam as he should. It was almost as though he had avoided getting to know everything about him. Maybe because he still felt Paul's betrayal so keenly.

That wasn't fair to Liam, or to him, really. Liam was a good guy. One of the best. Mark knew he could trust him with his life, he just hadn't truly trusted him with his friendship. Sad, but true. And something he vowed to change. They'd been partners for almost two years. He should know if the man drank tea.

"Why don't we drop you home?" Liam said.

Mark turned his attention back to the other two. Rebecca was handing Liam a bag, presumably with tea in it.

"If it wouldn't be too much trouble," she said.

"None," Liam assured her.

Mark shook his head. He didn't have to be a detective to tell that the chemistry between the two of them was intense. Liam should know better than to get involved with her until after the case was closed. Given how little they had to go on, though, that might well be never unless they caught a lucky break. And there was no way that kind of fire was going to be contained indefinitely.

Five minutes later they were in the car and driving to her house. It was just a short distance away, as she had told them. Liam walked her to the door while Mark stayed in the car, trying not to watch as the two said goodbye to each other. When Liam finally returned to the car he was grinning like he'd never stop.

Mark started the car and pulled away from the house. "So, you like her," he commented.

"She's really nice, a responsible citizen, what's not to like?" Liam asked, trying to sound casual and failing miserably.

"And she's pretty and I thought you were going to kiss her on the spot, you were so smitten," Mark said.

"I was not," Liam protested.

"Sure. Five more minutes and I bet you'd have proposed," Mark teased. "What I have to know is this. Do you actually like tea? Because, you know, if you go after her you're going to end up drinking a lot of it I have a feeling."

"I do like tea," Liam said. "She had a very nice selection of oolong, but I ended up going with the vanilla Earl Grey. That one's hard to find."

"How do you know that?" Mark asked.

"My grandfather was a tea drinker."

"The one who collected guns?"

"Yup, that one."

"He had to have been something," Mark said.

"You have no idea," Liam answered.

"Just do me a favor and be careful. She is a witness."

"I know," Liam said with a sigh. "You know I don't know how many times I've driven by that shop. Always meant to go in. I'm kicking myself now that it took a homicide to get me in there."

"You wouldn't be the first couple brought together by a dead body," Mark said, thinking of Cindy and Jeremiah.

As if on cue his phone rang. He pulled it out of his pocket and saw that it was Jeremiah calling. He answered. "Rabbi, what can I do for you?"

"You can tell me where they're going to sequester the jurors for the Jason Todd trial," the other man said, his voice quiet.

Mark knew that when Jeremiah got quiet it was not a good thing. "Oh no, please don't tell me."

"Yes, Cindy's on the jury."

Mark swore under his breath. "I'll find out where and get back to you. I've been trying to avoid the whole thing as much as possible."

"Hurry."

"I will, just don't do anything I wouldn't do."

"No promises."

The rabbi hung up.

"Cindy landed on the jury," Mark informed Liam.

Liam shook his head. "And just when we thought things couldn't get more complicated with this trial."

"Yeah, I know it's crazy, but I've got a terrible feeling in the pit of my stomach. If Cindy's on that jury then something is going to go horribly, horribly wrong. I just hope we're all ready for it when it happens."

4

Cindy was nervous as she arrived at the hotel. She was also stunned to realize that it wasn't just an ordinary hotel that they were staying at. Instead they were staying at the resort hotel that was next to The Zone theme park. The hotel, called The World, was by far the fanciest one in the area and she was shocked that the court was paying for such elaborate accommodations. She'd expected an out of the way budget motel stay, not this.

As her police officer escort drove down into the parking structure beneath the hotel, though, she started to understand. He had to pass the security gate at the front, showing the guard there his identification and his badge. Then they drove to the back of the parking structure where there was yet another guard. Once past him they entered a mini parking area isolated from the rest of the garage that could accommodate about a dozen cars. A couple other police cars were already there.

"This is the entrance they reserve for celebrities to protect their privacy," the officer told her. "There's a private elevator that only accesses the floor you'll be staying on. The owner was nice enough to donate the space. We'll be taking over the entire top floor of rooms and we have dedicated staff for the duration of the trial."

"Wow, that's like really, really secure," Cindy said, impressed and intimidated at the same time. "Is that normal?"

The officer hesitated and she turned to look at him. He shook his head slightly. "Look, I know you're a friend of Mark's and you've done a lot for the department. I'll level with you, but please don't spread it around."

"I won't," she said.

"Normally a sequester is just to keep a jury from being tainted. In this case, though, we're also trying to keep the press…and others…from harassing you."

"What others?" Cindy asked.

He frowned. "I'm not supposed to tell you this, but there have been some safety concerns. There have been two attempts on Todd's life and we just want to make sure that no one is crazy enough to go after anyone else related to this whole mess."

Cindy felt her blood run cold. Maybe Jeremiah had been right to worry was the first thing that rushed through her mind. She forced herself to take a deep breath. It was just an overabundance of caution on everyone's part. She could see why someone might try to kill Jason Todd, but going after the jurors made no sense.

Death doesn't always make sense.

Like a phantom from her past the thought reared its ugly head and she struggled a moment with the panic that ensued.

"Are you okay?"

"Yes, sorry. I'm fine," she said, forcing herself to take a couple of deep breaths. Everything was going to be okay. She was not a child, she was not alone, and the police were just being overly cautious.

They got out of the car and she grabbed her suitcase from the back. Then they entered a large elevator. Just as he had said, it had only two destination buttons inside: P and 12. There was a smaller button above the 12 but she wasn't sure what it was for. As an extra layer of security there was a card slot and the police officer pulled a card out of his pocket and inserted it in before they were able to successfully push the button for the twelfth floor.

"Will I get one of those?" Cindy asked.

He shook his head. "Only officers will have the elevator access cards as an extra layer of precaution."

Meaning that once on the twelfth floor she was trapped unless she had a police officer to escort her down. This hotel stay was beginning to feel a lot more like a prison sentence.

"What happens if there's an emergency?" she asked.

"Well, as they always say, in case of emergency take the stairs. And don't worry, we'll have officers stationed on the floor to unlock the doors if that happens."

It was going to be trickier for Jeremiah to keep tabs on her than she had thought, and she was beginning to feel like an idiot for telling him not to worry.

"Trust me, the rooms are so nice, you're never going to want to leave," the officer said with a smile that was meant to be reassuring.

For some strange reason an old song about a cursed California hotel that the guests couldn't leave came to mind and she shuddered involuntarily.

The door opened and they stepped out onto the twelfth floor. Cindy just stared in surprise. It didn't look like any hotel she had ever seen. She was staring at a massive open space shaped like a large rectangle. Straight ahead of her, in the middle of the space was what looked like a living room with couches set up in a square. Several board games were stacked on a table in the center. To the right was a library area with half a dozen bookshelves crammed with books and several comfy looking chairs with small tables next to them. To the far left was a pool table surrounded by several chairs and there was a single table with a phone on it.

"These are all common areas for you all to share," the officer explained. "If you need to make a phone call you can do so there," he said, pointing to the phone she'd already seen. She was relieved. He'd made her leave her cell at home which had made her feel very uncomfortable. At least this way she would be able to get ahold of Jeremiah.

He gestured to corridors at the far end of the room on each side. "Those lead to the rooms, eight on each side. We'll have officers in a room on each wing."

"This is crazy," she said, lacking another word to describe it.

"Your room is this way," he said, heading toward the side with the library. The corridor was past the last shelf of books. They stopped in front of a room emblazoned with the number three. He handed her a room key and a moment later she was stepping into the space that would be home for the next couple of weeks.

It was about twice the size of any hotel room she'd seen before. There was a king sized bed and at the far end by the windows there was a dining table. Halfway between the two against the left hand wall was a large writing desk. She poked her head into the bathroom which was done in green marble with fluffy green towels and sported separate soaking tub and shower.

"Very nice," she murmured.

"There's a room service menu on the table. That's how you'll take dinner. If you want breakfast there's a menu that you can mark and hang on your door before midnight. Just so you know, the television has access to a wide variety of movies that you can choose from, but no traditional television channels."

She nodded and her stomach growled at the mention of food. She had barely picked at her lunch and she was definitely hungry.

"If you need anything, officers will be in room two on this side of the building, room fourteen on the other side. There will also be an officer in the common area at all times."

"You really aren't taking any chances," Cindy said before she could stop herself.

"No, ma'am, we really aren't," he said solemnly. "Have a good evening."

He shut the door, leaving Cindy alone with her thoughts. She couldn't help but wonder if she was the first juror to arrive or if others were already locked away in their rooms.

She headed for the table and grabbed the room service menu. Fortunately everything looked delicious. She quickly discovered, though, that since there was no phone in the room she'd need to head into the common area to call in her order. She tucked her key in her pocket and headed out of the room. The door didn't close all the way by itself and she pulled it firmly until she heard a click, and then ventured out to the common area.

The police officer who had escorted her had already settled into one of the chairs in the library area and was reading a book, a thriller by the looks of it, called *The Thirteenth Sacrifice*. She made her way over to the far side of the room and picked up the receiver on the phone. There were no buttons on it and a moment later a pleasant sounding young woman answered.

"Hi, I'm staying in room three up on the twelfth floor and I need to order some dinner."

"Of course. I can help you with that. What would you like?"

"The steak with béarnaise sauce, a Coca Cola, and some chocolate mousse."

"Excellent choices. I'll have them sent right up."

"Thanks."

"Is there anything else?"

"Yes, I need to call my fiancé."

"Certainly, give me the number and I can put you through."

Cindy told her, grateful that she had the number memorized. Seconds later she heard Jeremiah's voice.

"I miss you," were the first words out of her mouth.

"Not half as much as I miss you. I know where you are."

"Oh good," she said, glancing around. She wasn't sure if the officers would take kindly to her revealing that information. She doubted that the man across the room could hear her, though. Still, as a precaution she dropped her voice. "Three on twelve," she said, trusting him to figure that out.

"Way ahead of you," he said.

"Good. It's nice here, but I feel like I'm the one in prison," she admitted.

"If you need to arrange a jail break…"

"I know who to call," she said, smiling at the thought. She had a sudden image of Jeremiah dropping from the ceiling like something out of a *Mission Impossible* movie. "I better go get unpacked before my dinner shows up."

"Okay. I love you."

"I love you, too," she said, blushing happily even as she said it.

She hung up and headed back to her room. Once inside she opened the curtains and discovered that she had a view of The Zone theme park. The lights glittered in the dark and she was able to make out several of the rides. She sighed, wishing she was there having fun with Jeremiah instead of stuck in the hotel. She stood and watched the lights for another minute before beginning to unpack her things. She had just finished when there was a knock on the door. She opened it, half expecting to find a police officer delivering her food.

Instead a young waiter smiled at her over the tray in his hands. "I believe you ordered dinner?"

"Yes," she said, standing aside to let him in.

He moved over and put the tray down on the table. "You can put it outside your room when you're done," he said.

"Thank you. Is there a bill or something I need to sign for?"

"Oh no, ma'am, it's compliments of the hotel."

"Wow, that's very generous."

He shrugged. "It's our pleasure. Have a good night."

"You, too," she said as he quickly left.

She sat down and savored her food as she stared at the dancing lights of the theme park below. Her thoughts drifted as they often did to Jeremiah.

Part of her was still in shock that they were engaged. The ring on her finger was proof, though, and she touched it to her cheek as she sometimes did just to remind herself it was real. She had brought the bridal magazines with her since she'd have a lot of time on her hands. Maybe she could start to figure out what she wanted in the way of a wedding or a dress or a cake or anything.

The truth was whenever she tried to focus in on those details she lost herself in imagining what it would be like to stare into Jeremiah's eyes as they recited their wedding vows. Thanks to Geanie and Joseph's wedding she'd had a sneak peek of what that might be like. Every time she thought about it she felt excited and tingly all over.

Geanie had promised to take her dress shopping that weekend. Unfortunately it would have to wait until this whole trial thing was over. That was fine, though. Maybe that would give her time to think about what she wanted. She knew it would likely be a lot different than Geanie's dress. Long sleeved maybe, without ruffles, and maybe some pearls. Geanie's dress sparkled, but Cindy's dress should be softer.

A sudden crashing sound right outside her door drove her to her feet, heart pounding. She moved forward, determined to find out what was going on. If there was danger she would not be trapped in her room with no way out.

At the door she hesitated with her fingers touching the handle. There was a peephole and she looked through it, trying to get a sense of what was happening. She relaxed and pulled open the door.

There was a huge pile of luggage in the middle of the hall, two large suitcases fallen over half on top of smaller ones. A woman in an elegant black dress sat on the floor next to them, her face scrunched up in pain and staring at her hand.

"Are you okay?" Cindy asked. She vaguely recognized the woman as one of the other jurors she'd seen earlier that day.

"No, I'm not. I broke a nail and I'm pretty sure I twisted my ankle. Stupid luggage. I can't believe I couldn't get a porter. If we'd gone through the lobby like civilized people instead of skulking like criminals none of this would have happened."

Cindy bit her lip to keep from saying something less than kind about the broken nail. It clearly distressed the woman and she should be nice. She bent down and picked up one of the suitcases. "How about I help you get this to your room?"

"That would be lovely," the woman said, and Cindy couldn't tell if she was being sarcastic or sincere.

"Which room are you?"

"Six."

"Well, that's just a few feet away. You're almost there. If you want I can call room service and have them bring up some ice for your ankle, just in case."

"I broke my nail, but my wrist is fine. I can call them myself," the woman said stiffly, starting to get to her feet.

"The only phone is back that way, by the pool table," Cindy said, pointing. "There aren't any in the rooms."

The woman looked at her like she was insane. "You have got to be joking."

"I wish I was. If you want anything from room service, you need to call from out there."

"This is unacceptable," the woman said, bristling. "Don't you know who I am?"

"I don't make the rules, I'm just trying to let you know what's going on. And, frankly, no, I don't know who you are," Cindy said, forcing herself to smile at the end even though she wanted to glare.

The woman drew herself up to her full height. Her ankle must not have been as injured as she made out since she seemed to be unfazed as she stood there in her three inch designer heels. At least, Cindy assumed they were designer heels. She had a feeling the woman wouldn't tolerate anything less.

"I am Prudence Black."

"Hello. I'm Cindy Preston," Cindy said.

The woman stared at her, clearly expecting more of a response. "I said, I am Prudence Black."

"Yes, I heard you."

The woman gave a disgusted sigh. "My husband is mayor of Pine Springs."

"Oh," Cindy said. She knew that Samuel Black was the mayor, but she had honestly never heard his wife's name. "Nice to meet you."

The woman rolled her eyes and marched toward her door, her ankle holding up just fine. She left all her luggage piled there in the hallway as she opened her door and went inside.

Cindy just stood for a moment, waiting for the woman to come back out. When she didn't, Cindy headed toward the door, rolling the suitcase she'd picked up behind her. Maybe the woman had gotten inside and finally collapsed. When she crossed the threshold, though, she saw that Prudence was staring out the window at her view of a parking lot.

"Completely unacceptable," Cindy heard her muttering.

"Your ankle seems to be okay," Cindy said, unable to keep the sarcasm from her voice.

"What?" Prudence asked, turning. "Yes, it's fine. You can put the luggage in the closet."

Cindy bristled. "I'll put this one in there for you. Since you don't need any ice and your ankle seems to be okay I'll let you handle the rest."

Prudence looked nonplussed. After putting the bag in the closet Cindy turned to her and forced a smile. "It should be an interesting couple of weeks at least," she said.

Prudence just kept staring at her as Cindy turned and walked back into the hall. She nearly collided with the man in the blue work shirt who had been complaining that morning that it was his turn to pick up his kid from school.

"Sorry, miss," he said, giving her a tired smile. He had a battered, old suitcase in one hand.

"It's okay."

He turned and looked at the pile of luggage in the middle of the hallway. "Do you need some help?" he asked.

"No, those belong to Prudence. This is her room. I'm sure she'll retrieve her bags in a minute or two."

"Okay." He shifted his suitcase to his left hand and held out his right. "I'm Mike, by the way. Might as well get the introductions over with seeing as we're all in this together."

She shook his hand. “Hi, Mike. I’m Cindy.”

“Good to meet you,” he said, shaking her hand warmly. “Any chance you can tell me where we go to eat?”

“There’s a menu in your room. The phone’s out by the pool table. And I’d suggest the steak. It’s very good and the hotel’s paying for all the food,” she said with a conspiratorial smile.

His eyes lit up. “Now that’s a deal. I could go for a good steak right about now.”

“Well, enjoy,” she said.

“Thanks.”

He continued down the hall and she returned to her room, stepping over the luggage in front of her door. She grabbed the handle and realized she’d forgotten that the doors didn’t automatically close all the way by themselves. She’d have to remember that, she thought as she pushed open her door and walked inside.

She thought of all the policemen who were supposed to be on guard and took a deep breath. She had to remember that no matter how nice the room and how good the food, someone, at least, thought that they were in danger.

5

Mark made it home and walked in the door expecting chaos to greet him, but all was serene. Buster, their beagle, jumped off the couch and calmly walked over to sniff him. The twins were nowhere to be seen.

"Honey, I'm home," he called out as he reached down to scratch Buster behind the ears.

Traci emerged from the back of the house wearing a pretty blue dress that had to be new. He would have remembered seeing it before.

"You look amazing," he said, as he walked forward to kiss her.

"Thank you. You…don't," she said with a frown. "What's wrong?"

"We got a case that's not so much a case. In fact, without a miracle, we've got nothing. I hate that. I've already got enough of those kind of mysteries," he admitted.

"Well, don't worry. I'm going to make you forget all about it," she said.

"Oh yeah?"

"Yeah. I have declared it's date night."

"God bless Geanie and Joseph," he said. The couple were their go to babysitters.

“Actually, they’re not with Geanie and Joseph,” Traci said.

“Your sister? They live a ways away, but that’s okay.”

“No.”

Mark cocked his head. “Who’s watching the babies?”

Traci hesitated then said, “Jeremiah.”

For just a moment he thought she was kidding, but when she bit her lip slightly he knew that she wasn’t.

“You have an assassin babysitting our kids?” The words exploded out of him.

“Who else could they be safer with?”

“Umm, anybody?”

“Come on, be fair. He’s one of our best friends.”

“Yeah, and he’s a killer. And when he’s not killing people, people are trying to kill him.”

“It’s just for one night. It’s going to be fine. It’s good practice for him. One of these days he and Cindy might have kids. Besides, he needed the distraction.”

“What? A distraction from what?”

“From the fact that the city’s got Cindy locked up in a hotel. You realize he was planning to break in there tonight when I got hold of him?”

“Oh great, so now he’s going to take our infants along while he commits a felony.”

“You’re overreacting. Besides, I made him promise no felonies, misdemeanors only,” Traci said, suddenly smirking.

“You think this is funny?” Mark asked in amazement.

“A little bit,” she admitted.

Mark struggled with what to say next. Traci was the one who had made the decision, and while he honestly believed he was the more paranoid of the two, he had to admit that she would never put the kids in danger. And she was right. In this messed up world that they lived in they were far safer with their friendly neighborhood assassin than anybody else. He forced himself to take a deep breath.

"Okay. Where are we going?" Better to just focus on whatever entertainment Traci had planned for them than spend time imagining Jeremiah teaching his children about the proper way to hold a gun. As the image popped into his mind, though, it was so absurd that he almost started to laugh. Then he had a far more frightening and realistic vision of Jeremiah teaching the twins as a birthday gift when they turned five.

"We are going someplace where we can have fun and you can lighten up," Traci said.

Mark was on the verge of telling her that such a place didn't exist, but he forced himself to take another deep breath. This was a good thing she was doing. He had been stressed and on edge and blowing off some steam with his wife sounded like the perfect remedy.

"Do I need to change?" he asked.

"I'd say 'just your clothes', but why stop there?" she said, smirking.

He shook his head. "You are feeling feisty tonight."

She waggled her eyebrows at him. "You have no idea."

~

Jeremiah couldn't help but be amused. Rachel and Ryan were a little more than seven months old and they were curious about everything around them. Traci had been completely transparent when she'd asked him to babysit for the evening. He had called to ask her if Mark was going to be working late. He had been planning to break into Cindy's hotel, but only if the detective wasn't there. He had no need to make things awkward for the other man if he could help it. Plus, if he had been at the hotel, Jeremiah could have relaxed a bit more, trusting that Cindy would be safer.

Traci had instantly clued into what was going on and had asked him to babysit instead. He'd thought about declining, but in the end had realized that he was being rash and having something to take his mind off his own needless worrying would be a good thing. Besides, it was the first time Traci had asked him to babysit and even though he knew she had an ulterior motive he was still honored that she trusted him with her children.

The two were currently in his living room. They were playing intermittently with some toys, but Rachel seemed determined to try and stand up. Using the coffee table she would pull herself halfway up before falling back down.

"In a hurry to go someplace?" he asked her when she looked up at him.

She smiled but didn't make a sound. Ryan, on the other hand, wouldn't stop trying to talk. For a little guy he was able to produce an amazing range and variety of sounds.

Captain had been laying quietly in the corner, closely observing the tiny invaders. He watched every movement intently, but made only the smallest of movements of his own. The children had yet to even notice that he was there.

His cell rang and he pulled it out of his pocket, mildly surprised to see from the display that Joseph was calling.

"Hello, Joseph, what can I do for you?" he asked as he answered the phone.

"Hi, nothing really, just calling to you know, talk, catch up," Joseph said, trying and utterly failing to sound casual.

"Mark and Traci didn't want me to think they didn't trust me so instead of calling themselves they had you call, right?"

"Right," Joseph said, sounding sheepish. "I should have had Geanie do it. She's sneakier than I am."

"Sneakier, yes, more subtle, not usually."

"True," Joseph said with a laugh. "No one ever accused Geanie of being subtle about anything."

"Everything's fine here. No one's had to go to the hospital. No dead bodies have cropped up. All's quiet."

"That's a relief. I mean, not that I thought any of those things had actually happened. Although with your track record, I mean, our track record, you never know I guess."

Jeremiah felt himself beginning to smile as he listened to Joseph try to make things better and instead make things worse. Smiling and laughing were two things that weren't coming completely naturally to him still so it felt good, knowing that the smile was genuine and that he didn't feel the need to control it.

"Pine Springs does come in for more than its share of excitement. It's not what I envisioned when I signed up to live here."

"You know, to be honest, I don't remember it being all that exciting until a few years ago."

"You mean until I showed up?" Jeremiah asked.

"No, until that serial killer thing happened. That was after you arrived, right? I mean, it was, right?" Joseph said, a note of panic edging into his voice at the end.

"No, the day Cindy found that body was my first day at the synagogue, my third day in town," Jeremiah lied.

"What?" Joseph asked, sounding dismayed.

"I'm teasing you. I was here a couple of years before that."

"Well, that's a relief."

"So, do you and Geanie want to come over?" Jeremiah asked.

"Yes!" Joseph exclaimed. "Sorry, I mean, sure, we could do that."

Jeremiah laughed out loud.

"Can we bring anything?" Joseph asked.

"I don't have much in the fridge so if you guys want snacks you'll need to bring them."

"Done. We'll be there in a few."

Jeremiah smiled at the twins as he hung up. "Apparently Uncle Joseph and Aunt Geanie are coming over. Guess they just couldn't stay away."

Ryan cooed and Rachel seemed to redouble her efforts to pull herself up. Jeremiah got up and closed his bedroom door. He didn't need either Geanie or Joseph accidentally seeing the gun he had on his chest of drawers. Ever since coming back from Israel it had scarcely been off his person. With the twins in the house he'd made an exception, putting it in the other room and out of their reach. It made him uncomfortable, but he forced himself to live with it. No one, not even Cindy, realized that he was armed at all times. On the rare occasions he wasn't carrying a gun he was at least carrying a knife.

Geanie and Joseph showed up so fast he wondered if they'd called from the grocery store down the street. They carried bags with sodas and assorted chips and dips in with them.

Ryan clapped his hands together enthusiastically when they walked in the living room and Rachel seemed to forget all about trying to stand and crawled straight over to Joseph who picked her up.

"They like you," Jeremiah commented.

"I would hope so. We spoil them as often as we can," Geanie said.

"Mark and Traci are constantly threatening payback when we have kids, but let's be honest, they won't be able to afford it," Joseph said with a grin.

Joseph rarely talked about money and never bragged on having it, so to hear him say something of that sort surprised Jeremiah.

"Yeah, but I'm sure they'll think of other ways to outspoil us when we have kids," Geanie said. "They'll let them stay up all night and do obnoxious things."

"True," Joseph said as he sat down on the couch, still holding Rachel.

Geanie got the blocks from the bag of toys that Traci had sent home with Jeremiah and sat down on the floor with Ryan.

"You see," Jeremiah said. "Everyone's fine."

"Yes, we see that," Joseph said, giving Rachel Eskimo kisses with his nose.

"So, you two going to be trying for kids soon?" Jeremiah asked as he observed them.

Geanie and Joseph both turned and looked at him with blank stares. "I don't know, why do you ask?" Geanie said.

"Because you guys are obviously crazy about these two. I can see you starting a family of your own."

Joseph shrugged. "No need to think about that right now. We've got plenty of time," he said nonchalantly.

Jeremiah shook his head. “What did we discuss on the phone about you being lousy at lying?”

Joseph winced and looked back down at Rachel.

“We’re trying, but don’t tell anyone,” Geanie said with a sigh.

“That’s wonderful news. Don’t worry, my lips are sealed.”

“Thank you,” Geanie said.

“How about you and Cindy, have you picked a date for the wedding yet?” Joseph said, clearly trying to change the subject.

“Not yet. There is one thing that has been decided, though,” Jeremiah said.

“Yes?” both Geanie and Joseph asked in unison.

“Joseph, would you be one of the groomsmen?” Jeremiah asked.

Joseph gave him a huge grin. “I’d be honored. That would be awesome!”

“Are you going to ask Mark to be your best man?” Geanie guessed.

Jeremiah nodded. “That’s what I was thinking.”

“Good choice,” Joseph said.

Jeremiah glanced at Geanie. “I think Cindy wants to be the one to ask you something,” he said.

She waved her hand. “That’s fine. As it should be. Of course, if she even thinks about picking Traci over me for maid of honor then Traci and I will be having words. Or maybe even an arm wrestling competition.”

“Considering neither of you is a maid maybe she’ll pick someone else for that,” Joseph said.

“Nah. Maid of Honor, Matron of Honor. Either way it’s the big MH and I plan on it being me.”

"Not that you're even remotely competitive and forgetting entirely that it's Cindy's choice," Joseph said teasingly.

Geanie shrugged and turned back to Ryan and the blocks.

"Seriously, whatever you need us to do, we're happy to do," Joseph said.

"I appreciate that."

"How could we not? Both of you nearly got killed trying to see us safely married," Geanie said.

"Let's hope their wedding isn't as eventful as ours was," Joseph said.

"What are the odds?" Jeremiah asked, trying to be funny.

Instead both Joseph and Geanie turned and looked at him intently. "Probably not good," Geanie said at last. "We should plan for every possible contingency."

"I was joking," he said.

"Better safe than sorry. Don't worry, we're on it," Joseph said.

"On what?"

"Disaster preparedness plans for your wedding, of course," Geanie said.

"You know, we could book 3 alternate venues for the actual event. We could have limos pick up the guests at their homes and only tell the drivers at the last minute where they're going," Joseph said.

Jeremiah laughed and then realized that Joseph wasn't trying to be funny. "Are you serious?"

"It could work," Geanie said thoughtfully.

"Yeah, until someone impersonates a wedding guest or a limo driver," Jeremiah said. "Something like that only works if both parties are known to each other ahead of time."

There was a long pause and then Joseph nodded. "Good point. Maybe we should rent a private island for the weekend. That way we could completely control access, who gets on and off."

"Don't you think that's a bit extreme?"

"Not if it keeps you guys safe," Geanie said earnestly.

Jeremiah couldn't believe they were even having this discussion. He had to find a way to control this before the two of them spun completely out of control. "I think that's overkill, really I do. And besides, I've gotten onto a private island before...uninvited."

"Ooh, that sounds like a good story," Geanie said.

"And one you're not going to hear," he said firmly.

"Fine," she said, even though she made a slight pouting face.

"Seriously, I think what Cindy and I both want is a nice, normal wedding."

"That might be what you want. The question is, what will you get?" Joseph asked.

Geanie nodded. "You two do seem to attract trouble, particularly if it's a holiday or special occasion of any kind."

"Yeah, what is up with that?" Joseph asked.

Jeremiah sighed. Whether he liked it or not he had to admit that they weren't wrong. "Okay, maybe a little disaster preparedness planning, but quietly. I don't want Cindy to feel all weird or worry unnecessarily."

"You've got it," Geanie said. "Mum's the word." She picked up the blocks and spelled out mum. "You hear that

Ryan? Mum. No telling Aunt Cindy what we're doing. Your mom or dad either for that matter."

Ryan laughed.

"If Mark's smart he's already making his own disaster preparedness plans," Joseph pointed out.

Jeremiah sighed. He hadn't been ready for their friends to take such an active concern in the planning of their wedding. That was probably his fault. He should have known they'd want to be privy to all the details. And given how often disaster did strike around them it was only logical that they'd be thinking about all the things that could go wrong at his and Cindy's wedding.

Wedding.

He still felt the need to pinch himself every time he really thought about it. Sometimes he wondered if he was an idiot for thinking they could have a normal life. Then he'd stop, take a deep breath, and tell himself that it didn't matter. All that did matter was that they would be together. Forever.

"So, are you going to be okay for the next couple of weeks?" Joseph asked, snapping him back to the present.

"You mean while Cindy's got jury duty?"

Geanie and Joseph both nodded.

"Yeah, I'll be fine."

"You're not going to try and do something rash, are you?" Joseph asked.

Jeremiah rolled his eyes. "Traci told you?"

"Of course," Geanie said.

"No, I'm not going to do anything rash. Shouldn't you two be concerned, though? I mean after all, things could go wrong."

"That sounds logical."

"And this way we're close by if Jeremiah does anything rash," Traci said casually.

"Ah hah! I knew this had something to do with them. You *do* think he's going to break in here and bring our babies with him."

"No, not really," Traci said, a hint of hesitation in her voice. "But, you know, life can be unpredictable. I decided it couldn't hurt to be where the action, in the remote chance there is any, is happening."

"We're going to all end up in jail," Mark muttered as a doorman opened the door for them.

The man gave him an odd look, but didn't say anything.

The lobby of The World was spectacular, beautiful and elegant and with a distinct feel as if many different cultures were being represented. An all glass elevator had a sign above it that read: *The Top of the World*. They moved over to it and moments later they were zipping upward. The glass floor beneath their feet gave Mark a moment of dizziness, but it passed before the elevator slowed to a stop.

Traci sucked in her breath as they stepped out of the elevator and looked out the panoramic windows at the city with all its twinkling lights. "Oh, it's so pretty up here," she said.

And seeing the smile on her face he was glad they were there, even if potential drama could be unfolding just one floor down. He took a deep breath. He couldn't think about that. In fact, looking at his wife, he decided he was crazy and deserved to be shot if he spent the night thinking about anything else but her.

They were escorted a minute later to a table for two by one of the windows. Looking out at the twinkling lights it really did feel like they were on top of the world.

"Okay, so what's the deal with this place?" Mark asked once the waiter had taken their drink order and left.

"They serve dishes from all over the world. You can either mix and match or stick with a particular country or region for your entire meal. Geanie and Joseph told me they even have private themed rooms."

Dinner was delicious with Mark choosing an entirely Japanese themed menu and Traci going with a Russian one. They sampled liberally off each other's plates and had a great time. When they finally paid the check and were headed downstairs it was far too soon for him.

"Thank you, that was fun and relaxing. We needed that. I just wish we could have stayed there for another few hours," he said with a sigh as he fished the valet claim ticket out of his pocket.

"Oh, we're not finished yet," Traci said with a mischievous smile.

"We're not?" he asked hopefully.

"No. We'll leave the car in valet and walk to our next destination."

"We're not going into the theme park, are we?"

"Nope."

He reached out to take her hand, but let her lead as they walked away from the hotel and down the sidewalk.

Between the entrance to the hotel and the entrance to the theme park were several shops and a couple of restaurants. They passed them and Mark gave up trying to figure out where they were actually heading. Instead he focused on watching how the moonlight played across

Traci's face, bathing her in a silvery glow and making her look like even more of an angel.

"Here we are," she said, turning in toward one of the buildings.

He glanced up and noticed in surprise that it was a laser tag facility.

Before he could say anything Traci had hauled him inside. She had made a reservation and they were quickly shown into a room where they could gear up. Traci had her vest on and her weapon in hand lightning fast. Mark hesitated, though. This wasn't exactly his idea of fun.

"You okay?" Traci asked him, noticing he hadn't geared up yet.

"Yeah, fine, it's just...I play cops and robbers for a living," Mark said, struggling to hide his disappointment.

"Ah, but this isn't about being the good guy or trying to catch the bad guy. All those rules get thrown out the window because there's only one thing that matters here," she said, inspecting her weapon.

"What's that?"

"Total and complete carnage," she informed him with a vicious smile.

Mark blinked at her. "I can get behind that."

"I thought you could."

They moved into the holding room where the rest of the players were assembling. Mark stopped just inside the door. He was staring at a bunch of kids. His first thought was to wonder why they were out so late on a school night. His second thought was that he wasn't going to be able to do this.

"I can't, they're kids," he muttered to Traci just as a kid on the opposite team lobbed a spitball at one of the kids who would be on his team.

"Of course you can, because they're not *your* kids."

And it all clicked for him. As crazy as he was about his kids, he could take his frustrations over middle of the night diaper changes, lost sleep, and everything else out on the kids in that room.

"Lock and load," he affirmed to Traci.

Just then an employee entered the room. "Okay, everyone, let's go over the rules."

"Rules, we don't need rules," Mark muttered.

"Some people might," Traci whispered.

"...no hitting anything or anyone with your weapon, it is not to be used as a bat, people," the employee was saying.

Mark didn't know why, but he had a sudden urge to laugh. He glanced at Traci and saw that she was biting her lip. She was clearly feeling the same way.

A minute later they let the teams into the arena where they would have a few seconds to make their way to their own base as a starting point while they tried to acclimate to the pounding music and the dim lighting.

Mark was quick to notice that the kid on their team who'd had the spitball thrown at him seemed a little apprehensive compared to the rest. He wondered if the boy was used to being picked on. When the starting signal was given and Traci and the other kids charged forth, heading for the other team's base, Mark put a restraining hand on the boy's shoulder.

"Stick with me, kid, and I'll teach you to be a sniper."

The boy looked up with great, round eyes. "Really?"

"Yes."

And just like that Mark was thinking about Jeremiah and what the real life assassin was teaching his children. He shook his head and moved the kid to a position where they could watch every approach to their base but could not be easily seen by those trying to take it.

"Get ready, when you see one coming, fire at the sensors on their gun or chest, but keep down as much as you can. If they can't see you they can't shoot you back."

"Okay," the boy said, nodding eagerly as he crouched behind a large, fake boulder.

For his part Mark had found a crack in the barricade they were hiding behind that he could glance through. When he caught the first sign of movement his instinct was to bring up his gun and shoot through the crack. He kept himself in check, though.

"Enemy closing in. Should be in your sights in 3...2...1."

The boy had flattened himself on the ground and he peeked around the barricade and shot at the other kid. He hit him and it was all Mark could do not to shout with excitement. Even better was he could tell the other kid had no idea where the shot had come from.

Three more enemy fighters came into view and Mark felt himself grinning from ear to ear. "Oh yeah, we're going to have some real fun."

~

At seven-thirty in the morning Cindy left her room and walked into the common room. A couple other people were already there, including Tanner. She took a seat in one of the overstuffed chairs and waited for the rest to arrive so the police could take them to the courthouse.

She had tossed and turned all night, finally sinking into solid sleep an hour before her alarm went off. She hid a yawn behind her hand as she surveyed the others already there.

Aside from Tanner there was a woman in her sixties, one of those who had said she hadn't heard anything in the news about Jason Todd, and a man in his fifties who had dark brown hair that was slowly graying and a kind looking face.

He reached over, extending his hand to her and she shook it. "I'm Ezra Abram."

"Cindy Preston."

"Have you met the others?" he asked.

"Tanner, I've met," Cindy said.

"Then allow me to introduce Mrs. Joyce Stephens," Ezra said, indicating the older woman. "Joyce, this is Cindy."

"Nice to meet you, dear," Joyce said with a hint of a southern accent.

"We'll be spending a couple of weeks together, I figured the sooner we get to know each other the better," Ezra said with a warm, easy smile. "Joyce is a retired kindergarten teacher. Tanner works in marketing."

"I'm a church secretary," Cindy said.

"Ah, we're in the same line of work then," Ezra said with a smile. "I'm a rabbi."

"My fiancé is a rabbi," Cindy said, unable to suppress a smile at the thought of Jeremiah.

"Small world. Is he Messianic by any chance?"

"No, he's not," she said, feeling her smile falter slightly. "Are you?"

"Yes. I will keep him and you in prayer if you don't mind."

"I would be very grateful," she said.

She had never actually had an opportunity to really talk with a Messianic Jew and she found herself burning with a hundred questions. She forced herself to take a deep breath instead. No need to inundate the poor man right away.

More jurors arrived from the opposite wing to the one Cindy was in. One tall man who had to be in his mid-twenties was wearing khaki pants and a polo shirt with the Superman emblem emblazoned on it. He had a comic book tucked under his arm.

"Hi, I'm Ezra, I'm a rabbi," Ezra said, standing and extending his hand to him.

"Jordan Casey. I review comic books and other pop culture media."

"So, you're a critic then?" Ezra asked.

"More like a very opinionated blogger," Jordan said with a small smile. "This is Tara Jones, we met last night," he said, turning to indicate a young woman who looked barely old enough to vote. "She's a personal assistant. I think it's to some Hollywood type, but she's not talking."

"Hi," Tara said so softly Cindy almost didn't hear her. "I really am not at liberty-"

"Don't worry about it," Ezra said, clearly trying to put the girl at ease.

Cindy watched as an officer who had been standing at the far end of the room checked his watch then turned and started down the corridor. She saw him stop and knock on the first door he came to. It must be time to hit the road.

She glanced back toward the wing where her room was and saw Mike walking toward her, stifling a yawn.

"Did you sleep okay?" she asked when he got close.

"It wasn't the sleeping that was the problem. It was the waking up. Thought I had figured out the alarm clock, but apparently not," he said. "I wanted to be up early so I could call my kids before they were off for school. It's going to have to wait until tonight, though," he said.

"I'm sorry."

"Set a wake up call with the front desk, that's what I did," Ezra said cheerfully. "That way if you get up late you have someone else to blame."

"But, there are no phones in our rooms," Cindy said.

"I know. The front desk called the phone out here and the police officer who answered had to come wake me up," he said with a wink.

"That's practically naughty," she said with a short laugh.

The police officer who had gone knocking on doors returned to the common area. Several people trailed behind him. Ezra moved to handle introductions. There was a tall, handsome man in a business suit named Carson, a college Shakespeare professor named Viola, a pretty young actress named Rachel, and a tired looking woman in her forties named Lilian who mumbled something about how her family should have moved out of the area sooner. Apparently she was actually one of the alternates and was busy cursing her luck.

Two more men showed up, Stanley and Wyatt. Prudence was the last to show, looking quite put out about it, too. The woman was even rude to Ezra which just made Cindy's blood boil.

"Okay, everyone, we're going to head downstairs together," the one police officer announced. "Downstairs there will be 4 black sedans. Choose one and remember your driver because you'll have the same driver until this is over. They are responsible for you."

"They really aren't taking any chances," Ezra said softly.

"No, it seems not."

Once downstairs Cindy found herself in a car with Ezra, Tanner, and Rachel. The officer driving was named Monroe. Tanner was practically vibrating with excitement. Cindy couldn't help but wonder why he was so excited to be on the jury for the trial.

"You said you're an actress?" she asked, turning to Rachel.

"I'm trying to be," the other woman said with a smile. "I have to admit I'm a little panicked that I won't be able to audition for anything for the next couple of weeks. Then I take a deep breath and remind myself that it's not like I've gotten any acting jobs yet. A couple weeks probably won't make a difference."

"It's a lot better to think that way than to think about how you might be missing your big break," Tanner said.

Cindy turned and glared at him, surprised that he'd say something like that which could only upset Rachel.

Rachel took a shaky breath. "It will be fine. Besides, in three weeks I have an audition for a play I really want to be in. I'll just keep thinking good thoughts about that."

"I'll pray for you if you like," Cindy said, surprising herself.

"That would be really, really great," Rachel said. "Thank you."

Tanner rolled his eyes. "Lot of good that will do."

"Careful or I'll volunteer to pray for you and we'll just see what comes of that," Ezra said, turning around in the front passenger seat. The corners of his mouth were turned up in a slight smile but there was an intensity in his eyes that belied his playful tone.

Cindy decided that she definitely like Ezra a lot. Tanner, on the other hand, was becoming irritating and it was only day one of the trial. That didn't bode well.

She realized they were approaching the courthouse. She could see out through the tinted windows and saw people holding up signs outside the building. She felt herself tensing up as she wondered exactly how they would be running the gamut of protestors. Suddenly Monroe shouted. The car turned sharply and began to skid.

7

Rachel screamed as Tanner slid, slamming into her and pinning her against the car door. Cindy hung onto her door for dear life as her seat belt suddenly locked up across her chest. The tightness terrified her and she didn't know if it was that or the shock of the sliding of the car that was making it hard to breathe.

She heard what sounded like small explosions and her mind raced as she wondered if someone was shooting at them. The car straightened out for a moment only to suddenly fishtail and slide in the opposite direction. Tanner slid across the backseat and slammed into her, crushing her up against the car door. The car hit something with a sickening thud.

"What's happening?" Rachel cried.

"Hold on!" Ezra yelled.

Out the side window Cindy could see a massive tree looming up in their path and she realized in an instant that they were going to hit it.

~

"You're in an awfully good mood this morning," Liam commented.

"What makes you say that?" Mark asked as he pulled away from Liam's house after having picked the other officer up for their shift.

"You're humming."

"So I am," Mark said with a short laugh. "Traci and I had a date night last night and I can't remember the last time I had so much fun."

"What did you do?"

"Dinner and then we went to play laser tag."

"I love laser tag," Liam said.

"Given the arsenal you own that doesn't really surprise me. I know, you're not responsible for that, most of your collection you inherited from your grandfather."

Liam shrugged. "Mock if you want, but laser tag is a great stress reliever, as you clearly found out yourself last night."

"Yeah, I can't argue with you there."

Liam's phone rang and he quickly answered it. "Hello? We're about ten minutes out. Okay."

He hung up. "Hit it. We have to get to the courthouse now. There was an accident with one of the cars carrying jurors."

Mark cursed and slammed the pedal onto the floor. "And I'll bet Cindy was in that particular car."

"No bet. Knowing her luck I'm sure she was."

"Did they say what kind of accident?"

"No," Liam said, bracing himself as Mark took a turn fast enough to leave a layer of rubber on the asphalt.

Mark's heart was racing as he pushed the car past its limits. He was trying not to race ahead in his thoughts and imagine what they would find when they reached the scene, but it was impossible to keep images of Cindy in the wreckage of a car out of his mind.

"This is not happening," he growled.

"She's going to be okay," Liam said.

"We don't know that."

"She's a survivor. And she might not have been in the car that had the accident."

From the sound of his voice it was clear that Liam couldn't even convince himself of that, let alone convince Mark.

They made it onto the street that ran in front of the courthouse in record time and Mark had to stop the car. All around them was chaos. He saw a dozen police cars, a fire truck and an ambulance, not to mention what had to be a couple hundred people milling about in the middle of the street, preventing him from going any farther.

Uniformed officers were trying to herd people out of the street, but they weren't having much luck from the looks of things. He parked the car and got out. Liam followed suit.

"Can you see where the accident is?" Mark asked as he scanned the street.

"There!" Liam said, suddenly pointing ahead and to the left toward a small park across the street from the courthouse.

A black sedan was wrapped partway around a tree which had then fallen on top of the car, caving in the roof. Mark's stomach twisted as he stared for a moment at the wreckage, wondering how it could have happened. He walked toward it, unable to move faster because of the sheer number of people blocking his path. After a few steps he finally just started pushing people out of the way.

The first victim he saw was a young woman sitting on the ground whose badly bruised arm was being examined by a paramedic. Just behind her he could see a police officer on a gurney being loaded into the back of an ambulance.

He looked around frantically and saw paramedics looking over two men, one older and one younger who didn't seem to have anything immediately wrong with them. He had just started to breathe a sigh of relief when he saw Cindy.

She was sitting hunched over with her head buried in her hands. His stomach clenched as he rushed toward her. He crouched down on her right and reached out to touch her shoulder.

"Are you okay?" he asked.

She looked up, startled. "Yeah, I was just praying, thanking God for looking out for us."

"So, you're not injured?"

"Not as far as I can tell. They haven't checked me over yet, but I feel okay. Just shaken up."

"Oh, thank heavens. What happened?"

She shook her head. "I don't honestly know. We swerved suddenly, and then the car was just skidding out of control all over the place."

A paramedic walked over and crouched down on Cindy's other side. "Excuse me, I need to check her over," he said, glancing at Mark.

Mark stood and backed up a couple of steps. "We'll talk a little later," he told Cindy.

She nodded, then turned her attention to the paramedic.

Mark took a deep breath. He realized he had better call Jeremiah before the rabbi heard about the accident some other way. He moved a few feet away where there was a little less noise.

Jeremiah answered his phone on the second ring.

"Hi, it's Mark. Listen, I don't want you to worry, everything's okay. There was a little car accident outside the courthouse this morning. We're still sorting it all out. Cindy was one of the jurors in the car, but she's just fine."

"Good to know."

It took Mark a moment to realize that Jeremiah's reply hadn't come from the phone. As soon as he did, he spun around to find the rabbi standing right behind him, a grim look on his face.

"How on earth did you get here?" Mark sputtered.

"I've been here all along."

"What do you mean? How long is 'all along'?"

"Long enough."

"Did you see what happened?"

Jeremiah nodded and Mark felt his frustration levels skyrocket.

"Enough with the cryptic! Tell me what you saw."

"One of the demonstrators staggered out in front of the car. The driver swerved to miss him. When he did the tires blew out."

"The tires blew out?" Mark asked.

"Yes."

"All of them?"

"All of them. That's not the oddest part, though."

"What is?" Mark asked, convinced he wasn't going to like the answer.

"It looked to me like the demonstrator was pushed in front of the car."

"Seriously?"

"Yes."

"You think someone was trying to kill him?"

"No, I think someone was trying to get the driver to react the way he did. It was the last car down the street which had otherwise been closed to traffic. It was a few feet behind the other three. I think someone wanted that car to swerve into the other lane."

"But why? Since the road is closed to all but official police traffic there was nothing to be gained by getting the driver to swerve. It's not like there was oncoming traffic."

"I'm guessing if you inspect the car you'll find that the tires blowing out was no accident. They probably have some sort of spikes embedded in them which someone could have planted in the other lane."

Mark felt a chill touch him. "What possible motive could someone have? I mean, they wouldn't even have known which jurors were riding in which car. So, why randomly attack one of the cars?"

"To delay the trial, cause mischief perhaps."

"You don't believe that," Mark said, staring intently at Jeremiah.

"The accident would have served as a brilliant diversion. Everyone rushes over here and no one's paying attention to what's going on across the street anymore."

"At the courthouse."

"At the courthouse," Jeremiah affirmed.

Mark turned to look at the building. "There are an hundred reasons why someone would want unfettered access to that building, most of them having nothing to actually do with this trial."

"Exactly. If whoever caused this wasn't motivated by the trial then trying to figure out what they wanted and where they might have gone could pretty much prove impossible," Jeremiah said.

"There were guards inside, though. Someone would still have to slip past them."

"The guards were the first responders. Two went to pull people from the wreckage and the other two started working crowd control to get people away from the wreckage."

"Tell me you're joking."

"I'm afraid not," Jeremiah said.

"Given that you were here I'm surprised you didn't help pull people out of the wreckage," Mark said, realizing Jeremiah didn't seem to have made his presence known to anyone, even Cindy.

"I was trying to watch, to see who might be moving in an unexpected way after the accident," Jeremiah said.

"Any luck?"

"Not much. Like everyone I was staring at the car as it spun out of control. That would have been when someone would have made their move."

"But you got something, right? Knowing you, there has to be something you picked up on," Mark said.

"Three of the demonstrators who I saw before the accident didn't stick around afterward. There were two men and a woman."

"Can you describe them to a sketch artist?"

"There's no need," Jeremiah said. He gestured toward a news camera emblazoned with the logo of one of the local stations. "They were taking video of the crowd before the accident. I'm pretty sure we just need to borrow their footage and I'll be able to identify the three off that."

"Maybe the guy who got pushed saw who did it," Mark said.

Jeremiah shook his head. "He tried to get out of the way of the car, but was hit when the tires blew. He was unconscious but alive and they've already taken him to the hospital."

"We'll have to put a guard on him. Hopefully he'll come to soon."

"Hopefully," Jeremiah said.

"Okay. Now to figure out if someone is in the courthouse who shouldn't be," Mark said.

"You'll want to hurry," Jeremiah said. "Because if someone did sneak in there it was most likely either to steal something or to destroy something."

Mark felt his blood run suddenly cold. "The jurors from the other three cars. They should have moved them inside the courthouse already for their protection."

"Might want to rethink that strategy," Jeremiah said softly.

They were both being paranoid, that's what Mark kept telling himself. Yet, over and over again he had terrible visions of a bomb going off in the courthouse. It was ridiculous. They weren't trying some member of a criminal or terrorist organization. This was a computer guy who had killed his wife. Things like that happened every week.

And yet other people who killed their spouses didn't end up with credible death threats and scores of demonstrators at their trials. He looked around at all the milling people. So much chaos already it would be easy to create more and to slip away unobserved.

In that moment he realized he didn't even know where the family members of the victim were. Nobody had been talking about them. It was possible one of them was out for revenge and didn't trust the legal system to mete out justice.

Liam arrived just then, looking grim.

"What is it?" Mark asked.

"This wasn't just an accident. They found metal spikes embedded in the tires and some more on the road."

"Just as he thought," Mark said, indicating Jeremiah.

"You saw what happened?" Liam asked.

"He saw enough. We need to grab that camera crew and set up somewhere for Jeremiah to look over footage of the crowd." Mark took a deep breath. "And we need to evacuate the courthouse and search it from top to bottom."

~

Cindy had finally finished answering the paramedic's questions to his satisfaction when she glanced up and noticed a number of police officers running up the steps of the courthouse. From the looks of them something was definitely wrong and the hair on the back of her neck stood on end.

"What's going on?" she asked.

"With you? You seem fine. If you have any stiffness or pain that comes on in the next few days you should see your doctor," the paramedic said.

"I wasn't talking about me," she said, but then realized the paramedic wasn't even paying attention to what was happening around them.

She stood. Her knees were a bit shaky, but they held her up.

"Ma'am, you should rest a few more minutes."

She turned her head and saw Mark talking to a news crew. She wanted to go ask him what was going on, but the last thing she wanted was for a reporter to try and interview her about being a juror or about the car accident.

It wasn't an accident.

The thought popped into her mind and she would have instantly dismissed it if it weren't for the memory of watching those officers swarming into the courthouse. Something was definitely going on.

She stood, torn. The officer who had been in charge of her group had been taken away in an ambulance and no one had stepped up to claim responsibility for them. She glanced over at the other three jurors. Rachel was in the worst shape. Her arm was badly bruised from where she had been slammed into the car door by Tanner when he went flying. Tanner and Ezra both seemed okay. Ezra was sitting quietly talking with Rachel as the paramedics finished up with her. Tanner was pacing, nervous excitement in every line of his body.

Cindy didn't know what to do and with the uncertainty she could feel her agitation growing. She felt exposed and vulnerable and also felt a sense of responsibility for the other jurors. They had likely never been in a situation like this one before.

She moved over to Ezra and Rachel and sat down next to Ezra. "You okay?" she asked.

He nodded. "I have God to thank for that."

"You were in the front seat. Did you see what happened?"

"This guy flew out in front of us, from out of nowhere. It scared me half to death. The officer swerved to avoid him. Then something went wrong. It felt like the tires exploded. I think we ended up hitting the guy after all."

Cindy nodded. She'd thought it felt like they hit something before they hit the tree. She glanced back over at Mark, hoping he would look her way and she could signal him over. He was still intently talking to the news crew, though.

She sighed and turned back to Ezra.

"Heck of a start to jury duty, don't you think?" he asked with a wry smile.

"It would be a heck of a start for anything," she said. "Did you notice anything else that-"

Before she could finish her sentence she heard a shout from across the street. She looked up to see several uniformed officers running out of the building, herding other members of the jury in front of them. Something was terribly wrong.

She glanced over at Mark who had turned at the commotion and who was now running to meet the others. She took off after him, hoping to find out what was going on.

They had both made it to the far sidewalk just as the others made it down the courthouse stairs.

"We found a package," one officer said, gasping for breath.

"What kind of package?" Mark asked sharply.

"It's a bomb!"

8

Jeremiah had been trying to keep a low profile. He hadn't wanted Cindy to know that he was there. It was stupid, really. He hadn't wanted her to feel like he was spying on her and that he was going to be one of those husbands who monitored his wife's every move.

He'd had a bad feeling about this whole situation, though. The worst part was he hadn't been able to tell if it was his usual paranoia over her safety or if there was something really wrong.

He had his answer.

Looking through the footage of the demonstrators would have to wait. He darted across the street and came up behind Cindy and Mark. Cindy turned and her eyes grew wide in surprise. A moment later she had thrown her arms around his neck.

"We've got to move everyone back!" Mark was shouting to the officers and anyone else who happened to be listening.

He didn't have to tell Jeremiah twice. He bent slightly and scooped Cindy up in his arms and ran back across the street to the tiny park. When he set her down she appeared shocked.

"When did you get here?"

"A while ago."

Others were flooding their way, driven by several police officers. Some people were screaming in fright. With every moment that passed there was more chaos. People were milling all around, demonstrators, journalists, and jurors mixing together.

It was the perfect cover for an assassination. Jeremiah turned his head, sweeping the crowd, looking for anyone who was out of place, not acting like the rest.

Cindy noticed his stance. "What's wrong? What are you looking for?" she asked.

"A wolf among sheep," he replied shortly.

He kept his eyes moving. It was possible that he was wrong, but it didn't feel like it. The very air itself seemed charged, as if waiting for something to happen.

Two police officers looked like they were trying to round up the jurors. Two of the ones who had been in the car with Cindy were standing with them along with half a dozen others. The younger man who had been in Cindy's car was fifteen feet away, talking intensely with the reporter standing nearest them. They were quiet enough that Jeremiah couldn't make out what they were saying. A woman Jeremiah thought was the mayor's wife was shouting at one of the police officers, her face turning bright red during the exchange.

Then he saw what he was looking for. A man wearing a hoodie was walking away from him, pushing through the crowd with a singularity of purpose. He didn't stare across the street at the courthouse like everyone else, he just kept moving in a hurry.

Jeremiah took a step forward, intent on following him, when suddenly the reporter near Jeremiah clutched his chest and collapsed forward onto the juror he'd been talking to.

~

Everything happened so fast that for a moment Cindy had no idea how to react. Jeremiah took off through the crowd right as a reporter collapsed on top of Tanner.

"Help, paramedics!" Tanner shouted as he struggled to keep the other man from falling on the ground.

Cindy ran over and was able to help him lower the man down onto the street.

"What happened?" she asked as a paramedic appeared beside them.

"He grabbed his chest. Heart attack I guess?" Tanner said, eyes wide.

Cindy backed off a few steps to give the paramedic room to work. She turned and looked to see if she could find where Jeremiah had gone, but she couldn't spot him in the crowd. Something had to have sent him running off like that, though, and she wracked her brain, trying to figure out what it could have been.

Finally she gave up and turned back around just in time to see some police officers in heavy protective gear charge into the building. The bomb squad must have arrived.

She stood there and felt completely helpless. There was so much happening and there was nothing she could do about any of it. She looked back down at the man on the ground. She had no idea who he was or whether or not he was going to be okay. She did know that there was nothing she could do to help him and even just standing that close potentially put her in the way of the paramedics and whatever they needed to do. She looked past Tanner and saw that most of her fellow jurors were huddled together, looking shell shocked. Cindy moved toward them.

Joyce, the retired teacher, was doing her best to calm down Tara, the young personal assistant, who had tears running down her cheeks. Next to them Jordan, the comic book guy, was staring intently at the courthouse. He turned and glanced at her as she walked up. "You don't really think there's a bomb in there, do you?" he asked.

She shrugged. "I don't know. I hope not."

"This is crazy, like something you'd read about, not like anything you'd actually experience, you know?"

Cindy just nodded. She remembered feeling that way, but the truth was, crazy had kind of become the new normal in her life. She wasn't sure how it had happened, but it had. Staring at the stunned faces around her she realized that in some ways she had far less in common with them now than she once would have.

"Tragedy, it's all around us though we seldom stop to notice," Viola said. "It's a pity. A good tragedy can prove far more cathartic than a hundred comedies."

It made sense that a professor who taught Shakespeare would think in such terms. Still, it seemed a bit morbid to Cindy.

"I'll take a good comedy any day," Mike said as he walked up to them. "Life can be hard enough without depressing yourself with what you watch. Besides, I love hearing my kids laugh."

Viola rolled her eyes but didn't say anything.

"Comedy is harder than tragedy. To portray at least," Rachel said. Cindy noticed that the actress' arm was in a sling.

"Are you okay? I thought you were just bruised?"

"Paramedic said my wrist was sprained and that there was general muscle strain. He suggested wearing this for the next day or two."

"But not more than five days," Tara spoke unexpectedly, her voice a quaver. "You can't immobilize your elbow for more than five days without having problems."

"Really? How do you know that?" Jordan asked.

Tara just ducked her head and didn't answer.

"This is messed up. We need to just get this all over with as fast as possible."

Cindy turned around to see that Wyatt had spoken.

"What we need to do is make sure that we take our time and get this right, a man's life depends on it," Joyce said, glaring over the tops of her glasses at him.

"She's right," Mike said. "I don't want to be here just as much as everyone else, but we do have a responsibility to do this right."

Wyatt cursed under his breath and Cindy turned away, trying not to listen.

"I, for one, agree with Wyatt," Prudence said with a sniff.

Cindy hadn't noticed the arrival of the other woman and she jumped slightly.

"Please don't agree with me. I don't want to be on the same side as you in any debate," Wyatt said.

Prudence turned bright red and Cindy held up her hand in front of her mouth so people couldn't see her smiling. It was strangely comforting to know that she wasn't the only one Prudence had rubbed the wrong way.

"Do you know who I am?" Prudence asked, bristling.

"How can we not? You make sure everyone knows how important you think you are," Wyatt snapped.

A horn honked close by and Cindy and several of the others jumped. She turned and saw that an ambulance was trying to get past them and she stepped back to give it room. The others did the same. As soon as it had rolled past, Tanner joined them.

"That news guy is dead. Heart attack," he said.

And there was something really odd about his voice. Cindy looked closely at him. She had seen and even personally experienced a number of different reactions to someone dying, but she was having a hard time placing the look she saw in Tanner's eyes. Finally it came to her. He looked smug.

She found herself taking an involuntary step backward as she struggled to figure out what on earth would make him look that way.

"Did you know him?" she asked.

"No, why?"

He had spoken a little too hastily.

"You were talking to him, that's why," Viola said with a raised eyebrow. "Quite odd if you didn't know him, especially since part of the point of the whole sequester is to make sure we don't talk to the press."

Tanner hunched his shoulders slightly. "He was trying to ask me questions, but like I told him, I had nothing to say."

"Really?" Viola pushed.

"Really," he insisted.

Cindy took a deep breath. If personalities were already clashing before the trial even started it was going to end up being a difficult couple of weeks.

“What are the odds they’re just going to call a mistrial out of the gate?” Carson piped up. “I mean, enough crazy has already happened maybe they’ll just want to start over.”

“I don’t think we’re going to be that lucky,” Wyatt said.

“All bets are probably off if the building actually blows up,” Carson said.

“The pressure’s not on you since you’re an alternate,” Prudence said, addressing Carson.

“Doesn’t mean we still don’t have to sit and wait through all of this,” Lilian, the other alternate, snapped.

“It doesn’t do us any good to be at each other’s throats,” Mike said.

“No, it doesn’t,” Cindy added. “We’re all in this together so let’s just try to make the best of things and get through this.”

“They’re coming out of the building,” Jordan said, pointing.

Cindy looked across the street. Sure enough, the police officers who had rushed inside were now walking calmly back out. One of them was carrying a briefcase. She wondered if that was the thing that someone had decided could be a bomb. She doubted that they’d be acting so casual now if that was indeed what it was.

She watched as Mark and Liam moved to intercept the officers. Mark talked to one of them for about thirty seconds before pulling his phone out of his pocket and making a call. She was too far away to hear anything that was being said, and her curiosity was starting to get the best of her.

Mark put away the phone less than a minute later and turned to discuss something with Liam. She decided to go over and find out what was going on. She'd taken less than half a dozen steps, though, when one of the police officers from the hotel stepped in front of her.

"Jurors!" he called in a voice that commanded attention.

The steady hum of voices around her ceased as everyone turned toward him.

"Follow me," he said, then turned and marched toward the steps of the courthouse.

"It must be safe," Ezra said, appearing suddenly at her side.

"I guess so," she said.

She stared intently at Mark as they walked, willing him to turn around and come tell her what was happening. He remained deep in conversation with Liam, though, even as the group filed past him.

"-could have been pure accident," she heard Liam say.

Whatever Mark said in response she couldn't hear and she fought back her frustration. If it was important she'd surely find out at some point. In the meantime she was a juror, not an investigator, and that's where she needed to focus her energies.

~

Mark was frustrated and on edge. He was glad that the briefcase hadn't turned out to contain a bomb, but he still didn't like anything about this whole scenario. Supposedly the owner, a third year law student, had accidentally left it behind the evening before after sitting in on some proceedings. Why the janitorial staff hadn't found it the night before was a mystery to everyone.

And to Mark it was downright suspicious.

There was nothing else to do, though. The contents had been examined, the owner contacted, and the briefcase removed from the premises. Maybe Jeremiah was wrong about someone using the accident as a diversion to allow them access to the courthouse.

Since there was no one left inside and nothing else suspicious had been found the decision had come down to continue with the proceedings. If it had been his call he would have had the jurors back safe and secure in the hotel twenty minutes earlier. It wasn't his decision to make, though. Even if he was one of the ones who would have to live with it.

"Cindy didn't look happy," Liam noted after the jurors had gone inside the courthouse.

"Can you blame her? She's probably still rattled from the car accident. Something like that can have you out of sorts for the rest of the day. Then throw in the fact that she's got to be wondering if she's about to be blown sky high and I can just bet she's unhappy."

Mark looked around, realizing he had no idea where Jeremiah had gone. He frowned. He still needed the rabbi to go over that video footage and tell him who'd left the scene.

~

Jeremiah had found the hoodie the man he'd chased after had been wearing, but there was no sign of the wearer. Since he'd shed the garment out of Jeremiah's sight, he could easily have slipped back into the crowd unobserved.

He didn't like it. This whole thing felt like some giant setup. He just wished he knew what exactly was happening. One thing was for certain, he was going to be paying a visit to the hotel later to make sure Cindy was secure. He had been right to worry that the police wouldn't do enough to protect her. They were all just lucky she hadn't been injured in the car crash.

~

At last they were about ready to begin the trial. Cindy was seated with the others in the jury box. Ezra had been selected as the jury foreman which was a great relief to Cindy who really hadn't wanted that job.

Everyone was on edge. Even the judge was visibly tense. Still, things were beginning to settle down. The attorneys were present as was the accused, Jason Todd. There were a lot of people there to observe and most looked as agitated as Cindy felt. There was enough drama about this case without having everything go crazy this morning.

She took a few deep, cleansing breaths to try and calm herself and clear her mind. She wanted to make sure that she was focused and paying attention to everything that happened so she could draw solid conclusions about the innocence or guilt of the accused.

She looked at him. Jason Todd was a good looking man with auburn hair and high cheekbones. His suit was tailored and looked quite expensive. That made sense. He was, after all, a millionaire who'd made all his money in the computer industry. That was about all she knew about him except for the fact that he'd been accused of murdering his wife.

If he was innocent then he had to be in unspeakable pain. It would be bad enough to have the one you loved taken from you violently. To be accused of the crime, though, would be unthinkable.

As if sensing her gaze upon him, Jason turned his head slowly. He was smiling ever so slightly as he looked over everyone in the jury box. When he locked eyes with Cindy she felt a chill run down her spine and she barely suppressed a gasp. She had confronted many murderers in the last few years, but she had never seen eyes as cold and evil as his.

9

Jason Todd's gaze slid off of Cindy, but it left her with a cold, sick feeling in the pit of her stomach. She didn't have time to dwell on it, though. The prosecuting attorney stood up and turned to face her and the other jurors. The man stood straight. His salt-and-pepper hair gave him a distinguished look. He exuded a quiet sense of confidence just standing there. Finally, he began to speak.

"Ladies and gentlemen, over the next several days the defense is going to try to convince you that Jason Todd is a grieving widower who was unjustly accused of murdering his late wife, Cassidy Todd. They will try to convince you that theirs was a loving marriage and that he was so distraught in the days following her death that he must be excused for exhibiting erratic, downright guilty behavior. That is what the defense is going to try to persuade you is the truth.

"It's not. The truth is that Jason and Cassidy had a desperately unhappy marriage and that she was on the verge of leaving him when he murdered her. His actions in the days following her death were not those of a grieving man but rather of a guilty one. We will present evidence of the acrimonious nature of their relationship. We will speak with the divorce attorney whose services she engaged just three days before she was killed. Finally we will prove that no one other than Jason Todd had the motive, the means, and the opportunity to kill his wife and that he, in fact, did just that. Thank you."

The man stood for another moment, letting his words sink in, before turning and taking his seat. At that point the defense attorney stood, giving Jason's shoulder a squeeze as he did so. It was an act meant to comfort and reassure his client, but Cindy had a suspicion that he did it more as a show, to engender sympathy for his client. She took a deep breath, reminding herself that her job was to wait until all the facts were in before drawing any conclusions. That was going to be difficult given that she was ready to convict Jason just on the basis of the evil she'd seen in his eyes.

The attorney, who was younger than the other one, had dark, slicked-back hair and swaggered slightly as he approached the jury box. "Ladies and gentlemen. Life and death. At the end of the day that is all that matters. And that's what we're talking about here. Jason is not the villain here, as my colleague would have you believe. Rather he is the victim. First, his beloved wife was taken from him suddenly and violently. I'm sure each and every one of you can imagine how painful that must have been."

Cindy started slightly. She had been thinking exactly that before she'd had a look at Jason's eyes.

"To say that it disrupted his life and threw him into utter chaos is an understatement," the attorney continued. "Then, before he could even have a chance to process the fact that his wife was gone, came the horror of being accused of murdering her, the love of his life. His freedom, his dignity, even his right to mourn her were stripped from him. His very life was taken, utterly destroyed by the very people who should have been comforting him and seeking justice on his behalf. Now, everything rests on your shoulders. It is up to you to hear the testimonies and to ultimately give this poor man his life back. Thank you."

As the attorney returned to his seat Cindy glanced sideways at some of her fellow jurors, wondering if any of them had seen in Jason what she had seen. She noticed Joyce dabbing at her eyes. Something the attorney had said must have gotten to the former kindergarten teacher.

She caught movement out of the corner of her eye and turned her head to see one of the alternates, Carson, looking bored and checking his watch. With a start she realized it was a smart watch. Why would he bother wearing it unless he could use it to do more than just tell the time? If he was using it that meant he had to have a phone on him that it was paired to. How did he manage to slip those by his police escort the night before? She was torn between feeling responsible to report him and wanting to keep his secret in case she needed access to the outside world for some reason.

~

Jeremiah forced himself to leave the courthouse area and go to the Synagogue. He didn't want to, that was for certain, but he knew he was of no real help to Cindy while he was stuck outside the building and she was inside. He already knew that they were restricting who could be present in the observer section of the courtroom and that after the scare it looked like they were clamping down hard on that.

Not that they could stop him from getting inside if he made up his mind to. Trying to avoid just that, Mark had begged him earlier to go back to work and leave things alone. Mark wasn't the one engaged to Cindy, though. He didn't feel the burning need to watch over and keep her safe every second.

We're going to be together for the rest of our lives and I need to find a way to calm down, he thought. He couldn't spend every waking moment anxious about Cindy's safety. It wouldn't do either of them any good. The best thing he could do for both of them was relax, trust that if she needed him she'd find a way to get hold of him, and go back to work.

"Everything okay at the courthouse?" Marie asked as he walked in the door.

He wasn't certain but he thought her tone was just slightly less frosty than it had been the day before. Either she was getting used to the idea of him and Cindy together or she had heard about the accident.

"Cindy was in the car that crashed, but she's okay," he said, taking a gamble that it was the latter.

Marie made a tsk-ing sound. "That girl has the worst luck of anyone I've ever met."

Jeremiah was almost inclined to agree with her. He definitely needed to take his mind off of that, and, fortunately, he had an upcoming holiday to help. He pulled up another chair and sat down close to Marie who raised an eyebrow at him. He wasn't in the mood to be in his office. When he was on edge sometimes the walls in there felt stifling.

"What is it?" Marie asked.

"I just wanted to go over some of the Purim details with you," he said.

"Okay."

"We don't want a repeat of last year," he said.

"Absolutely not," she said, eyes bulging slightly from the memory.

"Yeah, we need to make sure we get people home before they pass out," he said.

"We've hired several shuttles that can take people home."

"Yeah, the trick is getting people off the lawn and into the shuttle."

"What do you suggest?" she asked.

"I don't know. Maybe we could cut them off at the bar at a certain point."

Marie shook her head sharply. "We tried that the year before you arrived. People just got belligerent. A fight nearly broke out. After all the mitzvah is to drink until you can't tell the difference between the names Mordecai and Haman."

"I know what the commandment says," Jeremiah told her. Mordecai was a hero in the Esther story and Haman was the villain who had tried to wipe out the Jews. "There still has to be a way to control things a bit better."

"If there is, I haven't thought of it," Marie said dubiously.

"Well, hopefully something will come to us," Jeremiah said.

"The bakery that we always get our Hamantashen from is pushing a new recipe this year that will use some strawberry preserves for the pastry."

"Instead of the prunes?"

"Yes."

"What did you do?"

"I ordered double, half of the new recipe and half of the old."

"Smart thinking," Jeremiah told her.

She shrugged. "I was planning on ordering extra anyway so we didn't run out like last year. It made sense."

Jeremiah took a deep breath. "You really do a lot of wonderful things here for the people. I want to thank you," he said.

She looked at him suspiciously. "And?"

"And nothing. Just, thank you."

"It's my job," she said briskly.

He stood up. "I know." He put the chair back where he'd gotten it from and headed for his office.

"You're welcome," she said, just as he reached the door.

He nodded, but didn't turn back around. He quickly settled himself into his chair in the office and looked at the stack of things already on his desk that he needed to address.

Marie really did do a lot for the synagogue and he didn't show his appreciation often enough. Sure she got under his skin frequently, but she was a good woman who truly cared about her community. Even if her community was limited in her own mind to just the members of the synagogue. He couldn't help but wonder if she'd ever accept Cindy.

He picked up the top paper on his stack and tried to read it. All the while, though, his mind was going over the events of the morning. He was still trying to figure out what had been the purpose behind the attack on Cindy's car.

He didn't think it had been personal against someone in the car because no one on the outside knew who was in each car. It was more likely aimed at interrupting the trial itself. He still wasn't entirely convinced, though, that someone hadn't used it as a diversion to sneak something into the courthouse. Whatever the reason, the spikes in the road proved that it had been a deliberate act.

The more he thought about it the more uneasy he felt about having left. Cindy could still be in very real danger. He wanted to race back there as fast as possible. He glanced at the clock. There were likely several hours before the court would adjourn for the day. If there was something amiss in the courthouse he'd be unlikely to find it while keeping his presence hidden. Not when it was full of people.

He'd return there later though and watch and make sure Cindy made it back to the hotel safe. That much, at least, he could do.

~

When they broke for lunch the jurors were led into a separate room where drinks and deli sandwiches were waiting for them. Cindy noted that they were being sequestered even here and not being allowed to go to the cafeteria in the building.

She grabbed herself a roast beef sandwich and a can of Coke then sat down at the table across from Mike. She unwrapped her sandwich as her stomach rumbled.

Tanner sat down next to Cindy. "Crazy day, huh?"

She nodded as she took a bite of her sandwich. “Kind of makes you wonder what’s going to happen next,” he continued.

“Hopefully nothing,” Mike said with a grunt. That was exactly what Cindy had been thinking.

“Yeah, but it’s all kind of exciting. I mean, what do you think that was all about this morning?” Tanner asked.

Cindy couldn’t help but stare at him. They both could have been seriously injured in that car accident and a man had had a heart attack in front of him. She would understand him being anxious, but his excitement was strange to her.

“I don’t want to talk about it,” she muttered.

“Well, how about the trial? What did you think of the opening statements?”

“We’re not supposed to talk about that,” she said, glaring at him.

“I know, I know, just curious,” he said, not sounding at all contrite. He glanced down the table. “Hey, Rachel? How are you doing after the accident?” he asked.

Cindy couldn’t hear what, if anything, Rachel said in response.

“Excuse me,” Tanner said, standing and heading down to the end of the table, presumably to talk to Rachel.

“What’s that guy’s deal?” Mike muttered. “He must be some kind of adrenaline junkie.”

“I have no clue,” Cindy said.

“But I don’t like ham,” Prudence whined loudly as she stood in front of the table with the sandwiches. The woman turned around. “Someone trade with me,” she said somewhat imperiously.

Cindy's grip on her sandwich tightened. She noticed that up and down the table people dropped their eyes, clearly also unwilling to trade with the woman. Who could blame them? Even if they might have been willing to give up their chosen sandwich, her demanding manner didn't make anyone want to do the nice thing. Quite the opposite, in fact.

"Someone just has to give me their sandwich," she tried again, eyes darting around the room.

"Have mine, I'm not hungry," Carson said with a grunt as he tossed it at her.

The sandwich hit Prudence in the chest and the woman began sputtering in outrage.

Cindy had to bite her tongue to keep from saying something. The guy had given her his sandwich. She could at least be nice to him.

As for Carson, he was standing in a corner of the room looking intently at his watch. He touched it a few times and she became more convinced than ever that he was using it to communicate with the outside world. She couldn't help but wonder just who that would be and what it was he was telling them.

From the far end of the table she heard Wyatt say, "I wish we could just vote now."

She sighed and barely stopped herself from rolling her eyes. Between Tanner's excitement and pushing, Prudence's rudeness, and Wyatt's very vocal desire to leave it could shape up to be a trying few weeks.

~

It had taken a while but Jeremiah had finally settled in and been getting some work done. He had gotten about halfway through the pile of papers on his desk when there was a knock on his door.

Before he could respond Marie poked her head in, eyes wide.

"What is it?" he asked, instantly on alert.

"Apparently a reporter at the courthouse this morning had a heart attack."

"I heard that something like that happened," he said, wondering where she was going with this.

"Why didn't you tell me?" she asked.

He looked hard at Marie. Her face was white as a sheet and she was shaking. He stood up swiftly and moved around the desk to her.

"Marie, what's wrong?"

"Were you there? Did you see it?" she asked.

He had seen the man collapse right as he was starting to chase after the man in the hoodie. He wasn't sure he wanted to admit that, though. "I saw paramedics rushing to help someone who had collapsed," he said. "I heard it was a reporter."

"The media, a bunch of jackals, all of them. They're supposed to be respectful, wait until people can find things out some other way than hearing them on the news. He was respectful, kind, the last of the good ones."

"Do you know him?" Jeremiah asked.

Marie nodded and a tear streaked its way down her cheek. "Isaac Bernstein. My brother."

Jeremiah couldn't remember her ever mentioning that she'd had a brother so the news surprised him. "Go, go see him, I can handle things here."

"That's just it. I can't see him."

"Why not?"

"They just reported everything on the news. He's dead."

10

"Oh, Marie, I am so sorry," Jeremiah murmured.

She took a step into his office, and he moved forward and hugged her. She buried her face against his shoulder and a moment later was sobbing uncontrollably. He prayed over her softly in Hebrew. He had never seen her weak, vulnerable, and it unnerved him somewhat.

She had a brother. All these years working together, Passover dinners spent at her home, and he had never heard about Isaac. There had to be a reason for it. Whatever it was, though, was being washed away by the flood of her tears. And he had been right there when Isaac collapsed and hadn't even really given him a second look.

A terrible suspicion flashed through Jeremiah's mind. What if the car accident had had nothing to do with distracting people so someone could break into the courthouse? What if it had to do with distracting people while someone killed the reporter?

Why, though? Out of all the reporters on that street, why him? He remembered that one of the jurors had been speaking heatedly with Isaac before he collapsed. He hadn't been able to hear what they were saying.

"I haven't even had a chance to call our parents yet," Marie said when her sobbing began to ease up.

"I'm sorry. It's just tragic," he said.

"It's suspicious," Marie said, stepping away from him and wiping in vain at the tears that covered her cheeks.

"It was a heart attack. There was a lot of excitement down there. These things happen."

"Not when it comes to you and that Gentile woman," Marie said with narrowed eyes. "Nothing ever *just happens*. Remember that driver who crashed into you two years ago? They said he had a heart attack, only it turned out he'd been murdered."

Jeremiah remembered all too well. He just wished Marie didn't.

"Marie, what are you saying?"

"I don't think he just had a heart attack. I think someone killed him."

Jeremiah stared at her for a moment, speechless. He'd had the same thoughts but he certainly didn't want to share that with her, not without more to go on. People could spend a lifetime looking for revenge when what they really needed was just to let go.

"I don't like this. I don't like any of it," Marie said.

Jeremiah cleared his throat. "Neither do I, but there's nothing we can do about it."

"Isn't there?" she asked with an arched brow.

"I'm not sure I follow," he said, working to keep his tone even.

"You and she are always investigating things. Why don't you call your policeman friend and get to the bottom of all this?"

"Marie, it was an accident, and even if somehow it wasn't, I'm sure the police don't need my help."

She snorted derisively. “They have more often than not.”

While he knew that wasn’t true he didn’t contradict her. Clearly she had her mind made up about all of this.

“I’ll tell you what, you go home and I’ll call Mark and see if there’s anything I can do to help.”

“Good,” she said. She hesitated a moment. “Purim-”

“Is the last thing you should be worrying about right now. Go, be with your family,” he urged. “Do you need me to drive you or call someone to pick you up?”

She shook her head and walked out of his office. He followed her and watched as she got her purse out of her desk. She started to shut down her computer, then stopped. “Everything you need to know is in the file called Purim.”

“Thank you. Have your husband call me when there’s more to tell. And I will do the same.”

She nodded and then without a backward glance made her way out of the office.

Jeremiah sat down on a chair and just stared off into space for a moment, gathering his thoughts and trying to remember everything he could about the moment he had seen the reporter collapse. Not the reporter. Isaac. The man had a name, a family, and Jeremiah knew them.

He pulled his phone out of his pocket with a weary sigh. Marie was right. He needed to call Mark.

When the detective answered the phone he sounded frustrated and tired. Jeremiah could relate.

“Do I even want to know?” Mark asked in lieu of a more traditional greeting.

“No, but you need to know. That reporter who had the heart attack this morning?”

“Isaac something. Yeah, what about him?”

"The news is reporting him dead."

"I'd heard."

"It turns out he was my secretary's brother."

Mark swore. "Marie has a brother?"

"Had, and it was Isaac."

"This day just keeps getting better and better," Mark said bitterly.

"For all of us."

"So, thanks for the heads up. Is there anything else you need?"

Jeremiah could hear Liam talking in the background and from the speed at which he was speaking he was guessing the two men were pretty much in the thick of something.

"Yeah. Marie thinks it might have been murder."

"Based on what?"

"I can't say for sure."

"Okay. You know what, looks like a heart attack, acts like a heart attack, I hate to say it, but-"

"I think he was murdered, too," Jeremiah cut him off.

Mark swore some more, his voice rising higher as he did so. Jeremiah hated to add to the other man's stress, especially when he had no proof. He couldn't even say it was a gut feeling. It was just that Marie was right. Accidents didn't tend to happen around Cindy and him. If nothing else, it would probably behoove Mark, and possibly the court, to know that one of the jurors had been arguing with Isaac before he died.

"Tell me more," Mark said after a minute.

"I don't have much. He was in a heated discussion about something with one of the male jurors right before he collapsed onto the guy."

"Do you know which one?"

"No, but Cindy would."

"And I can't get to her for a couple more hours at least. Great, just great."

"It could be nothing," Jeremiah suggested.

"Of course it's not nothing. It never is with you. And even if by a miracle it isn't anything, it's still something because our mystery juror shouldn't have been talking to a reporter in the first place. And with that reporter dead the only one who knows what they discussed is the juror. This whole mess just keeps getting worse and worse."

"Is there anything I can do from my end?" Jeremiah asked.

"I'm going to have to talk to the family, find out if Isaac had any enemies."

"I'll see what I can arrange."

"I appreciate that. Though to save time and effort I should just have you talk to them."

"You're the detective, not me," Jeremiah said.

"Yeah, well, if the whole rabbi thing doesn't work out for you..."

"Funny."

~

The prosecution had called their first witness to the stand, a woman in her fifties named Mrs. Miller who was a neighbor of the Todds. After she had been sworn in she took her seat and folded her hands in her lap. Cindy noted that the woman looked everywhere in the room but at Jason, studiously ignoring him.

She believes he did it, Cindy thought to herself.

"Mrs. Miller, would you be so kind as to step us through the events of the evening in question?" the prosecutor asked.

She nodded. "I was out jogging, like I am most evenings. I was just about back home when I passed the Todd residence, and sure enough they were at it again."

"Could you describe for the jury what you mean by 'at it again'?"

"Yes. The Todds would have these terrible, loud fights. They'd be screaming at each other and there was a lot of name calling and usually the sound of something glass or china breaking. Their bedroom window faces mine and sometimes they'd go on half the night and I'd have to put in earplugs so I could fall asleep."

"How often would these fights occur?"

"The last few months before that night not a week went by it seemed that they didn't have one. Sometimes it was more than once a week."

"And how was it on this particular night?"

"It was as bad as I'd ever heard it. Worse, actually. Only he was doing most of the shouting. He called her names I can't repeat."

"Then what happened?"

"I heard him shout, 'I'm going to take care of you once and for all.' She started to make this half-screaming, half-crying sound. That's when I knew things were bad and I called 911 from my cell phone. Before the police could get there, though, I heard shots fired. Then...then it was just quiet like you never want to hear," she said, her voice beginning to tremble.

"Your honor, I'd like to play the recording of that 911 call now," the prosecutor said to the judge.

The judge nodded consent and a few seconds later they were listening to the call which was slightly fuzzy.

"Please state your emergency," the operator said.

"My neighbors are fighting again, they're screaming, shouting. I'm afraid he's going to hurt her this time."

"Ma'am, are you calling on a cell phone?"

"Yes, I am. I'm standing outside 14 Goldfinch Lane in Santa Clara. I've never heard it get this bad. Please send someone, I'm afraid something terrible is going to happen."

Mrs. Miller sounded extremely agitated and distressed. Cindy found herself leaning forward, caught up in listening to events unfold.

"Who's going to hurt who, ma'am?"

"My neighbor, Jason Todd, he's going to hurt his poor wife, Cassidy."

"Ma'am, are you safe?"

"Yes, I'm standing outside their house, but I can hear them..."

On the tape Mrs. Miller trailed off then screamed.

"Ma'am! What's happened?"

"I heard gunshots! Gunshots! He's killed her."

"Ma'am? Ma'am? Hello, ma'am?"

"Hello, I'm still here."

"Ma'am, what's your name?"

"Helen. Helen Miller."

"Helen, I want you to get somewhere safe. Police and ambulance will be there within the next five minutes, okay? Helen, can you do that for me?"

"Yes, my house is next door. 12...12...my street is..."

Cindy winced as she listened to the woman on the tape struggling to cope with what was happening. Her heart ached for her.

“Helen, I’m going to stay on the phone with you until help gets there, okay?”

“Okay.”

“Can you see or hear anything else?”

“No...no. It’s quiet now. It’s never quiet over there, but it’s quiet now,” she answered, sounding dazed.

“Ma’am, I want you to get inside your house and stay there until help arrives. Can you do that for me?”

“Yes.”

“For your own safety stay in your home until an officer comes to speak with you, okay?”

“Okay.”

“Mrs. Miller, is that the phone call you made to emergency services?” the prosecutor asked as he turned off the recording.

“Yes, it is,” Mrs. Miller said, looking pained.

“What happened then?”

“I locked myself in my house, like she said. She stayed on the phone with me until I heard sirens outside. Then I hung up and waited for someone to come talk to me. The whole time I was so scared. I was afraid it was too late and that poor woman was dead. After about twenty minutes I peeked out through my curtains and could see that there were police everywhere and there was an ambulance parked in the street. It was at least another half hour or so before a detective knocked on my door wanting to talk to me. Detective Ackles was his name. I told him everything I’ve told you.”

“Thank you, Mrs. Miller.”

Cindy leaned back in her chair feeling like she herself had just been through the wringer. She felt so sorry for Mrs. Miller having had to live through it. It seemed clear that she'd been somewhat fond of Cassidy which had to make it all the harder.

The defense then took its turn asking her questions. He wanted to know if she always jogged at the same time of night, which she did. He wanted to know if she'd ever called the police before on Jason and Cassidy. She said she had once three years earlier, the first time she'd heard them fighting shortly after they had moved in next door. It had been very startling but since then she had gotten used to their fights though she always felt sorry for poor Cassidy because she felt that Jason was unfair to her and bullied her.

By the time he was done asking Mrs. Miller questions the judge adjourned the court for the day. Cindy felt a little bit of trepidation as they were shepherded down to waiting cars and whisked back to the hotel, but this trip was at least uneventful.

Back at the hotel she dropped her purse in her room and then made straight for the phone in the common area. She wanted a chance to call Jeremiah and she didn't know how many others were going to be wanting to call their loved ones, too.

Loved one, it was so nice to be able to refer to Jeremiah as that. That's what he was. And soon he would be family. She smiled at the thought even as she sat down next to the telephone. She dialed Jeremiah.

He picked up the phone so quickly she wondered if he'd been waiting for her to call, knowing that she would.

"How are you?" he asked, voice laced with tension.

"I'm fine. It was a stressful day, but I'm back at the hotel. I'm going to order dinner once I'm off the phone with you. How are things on your end?"

She stared in frustration at the police officer sitting just a few feet away. There were so many things she wanted to discuss with Jeremiah, but she knew she couldn't do so with the man listening.

"A bit rough. The police haven't figured out who attacked your car yet or why."

"I see," she said, struggling to keep her voice neutral.

"But trust me, we're all working on figuring that out," he said.

She couldn't help but smile at that. "Anything else I should know about?"

"Yes, actually. Things are going to be pretty chaotic for me in the next several days with Purim coming up. Marie had to take time off. Her brother Isaac died this morning of an apparent heart attack."

"Oh, that's terrible!" Cindy said loudly enough that the police officer looked over at her.

"Yeah, it was quite a shock."

"Poor Marie! You said he died of a heart attack?"

"Yeah, but as usual, things are a little more complicated than that. He was the reporter who collapsed this morning outside the courthouse."

"The one talking to Tanner?" she asked without thinking.

The police officer narrowed his eyes at her and cleared his throat.

"I'm not discussing the trial. A friend of mine's brother died this morning," Cindy told him.

He continued to stare at her, clearly a bit skeptical. She couldn't exactly blame him. Tanner wasn't a common name so the odds that she was speaking about someone other than her fellow juror were incredibly low.

"Yes, thanks, I didn't know his name to tell Mark," Jeremiah said.

"I'm going to have to go soon," Cindy said as the police officer continued to stare.

"Okay, but be safe. We're investigating the possibility that it might not have been a simple heart attack but that Isaac might have been murdered."

"I understand," she said.

"I promise you, whatever's going on, we will get to the bottom of this."

"You always do. Okay, I have to go. I love you."

"I love you, too."

"Give my sympathies to Marie. If that wouldn't upset her too much I guess, since she doesn't like me," Cindy finished.

"I will."

"Goodnight."

"Goodnight."

After hanging up with Jeremiah Cindy ordered room service. She ate and after she finished realized that she was exhausted. She got ready for bed and with nothing better to do she decided to call it a night.

~

Cindy yawned as she sat in one of the chairs in the center of the floor close to the mini library. She had barely gotten any sleep the night before, and she kept wondering how she was going to keep from falling asleep during the middle of the trial. Maybe when she got to the courthouse she'd grab a soda from one of the vending machines. A shot of caffeine might help.

She'd gone to bed early, but then had the worst time trying to fall asleep and when she finally had she then woke up every hour or so. It had gotten so frustrating after a few hours.

She looked slowly around, noticing that most of the others seemed subdued as well even though most of them at least looked like they had gotten some sleep. She counted bodies and realized there was someone missing although she couldn't quite think of who it was.

She stifled another yawn as a police officer headed down the wing of the hotel where her room was. She idly watched him as he passed her room and several others until he was standing at the far end of the hall. He stood there for several seconds and then she could hear the sound of him pounding on the door.

"Someone's a heavy sleeper," someone commented.

"I think he stayed up late. He had the television on loud until after midnight," Tanner commented with a yawn. "I know it kept me up. I don't know how anyone could sleep through that."

"The cop is going into the room," Carson said.

He was right. The officer was pushing open the door. Cindy got to her feet, the hair on the back of her neck standing on end. Something wasn't right.

Around her the other jurors seemed to sense the same thing. Conversations ceased and those who were sitting stood and turned, clearly trying to get a better look at whatever it was that was happening.

Seconds later the officer emerged from the room. He was speaking into his radio as he walked quickly toward them. Just as he reached them the elevator opened and four officers rushed out. Two headed down each hallway, armed with keycards.

"What's going on?" Cindy asked as an officer opened her room and walked inside. Seconds later he walked back out, closing the door behind him.

"Hey, why are they going into my room?" she heard Viola ask. "What are they looking for?"

"We're looking for Wyatt," the police officer standing near them said. "He's disappeared."

11

Mark was giving into the oldest cliché there was. He was buying coffee and donuts. What made it worse was that he wasn't the only cop there. The donut shop was one of the only places open for early breakfast close to the courthouse. While they also served breakfast sandwiches, he knew there was no use even trying to talk himself into one when he was staring right at a boysenberry jelly donut. He loved those things and this shop was the only one that sold them.

He had just finished placing his order when the cops at the tables all around him suddenly started moving, grabbing their coffees and heading en masse to the door. He turned just in time to see Liam fighting his way upstream.

"What's happened?" Mark asked.

Liam stepped close to him and dropped his voice. "One of the jurors has disappeared from the hotel."

"Don't tell me it's Cindy," Mark said as a chill raced down his spine.

"It's not. It was one of the guys. He was there last night. This morning he was gone."

"How?"

"They don't know yet."

"We better get over there," Mark said.

The server handed him his coffee and a bag with his donuts and he started toward the door.

"Not us. We're needed elsewhere," Liam said.

"That sounds ominous," Mark said, taking a sip of the scalding coffee.

"Someone found a body."

"You know what? As long as we don't know the body and we don't know the person who found it, I'm good."

"An anonymous tipper called it in, so we're probably safe there."

"That's a relief."

"As to the body, it sounds like it might be a tad hard to identify."

Mark grimaced as he spilled some coffee on his tie. "Great."

"Sufficient unto the day is the evil thereof," Liam said.

"What does that mean?"

"It's from the Bible. It means, don't worry about it ahead of time, just deal with the moment."

Mark stared at him over his coffee cup. "Since when did you start quoting the Bible?"

Liam shrugged. "It was my favorite verse growing up. My grandmother used to quote it all the time."

"In that case I'll do my best to make her proud," Mark said a little sarcastically.

"She's in heaven now. So, I'd worry more about pissing her off lest she talk God into throwing a lightning bolt at you."

"You have an interesting family."

Liam laughed. "You have no idea."

"Fair enough. Okay, let's go take a look at this body."

Mark made Liam drive so he could at least eat his donuts in peace. He had just finished the last one and was attempting to get the stickiness off his hands when they pulled up to an empty field that had a large sign at the front of it announcing the upcoming building of townhouses on the property.

As Mark got out of the car he took another glance around the area. “Advantage to dumping a body out here is there doesn’t seem to be any surveillance cameras anywhere nearby to catch you in the act.”

Liam raised an eyebrow. “Don’t get any ideas.”

A couple of uniformed officers and a forensics guy named Vaughn were already on scene and standing in the field about twenty feet away from the road.

As they walked up Mark was about to greet Vaughn, but his eyes fell on the body and he came to a halt, suddenly lacking words.

“Yeah, not pretty,” Vaughn commented, clearly noticing his reaction.

The hands and head were missing. Which would explain Liam’s cryptic comment from the donut shop.

“Someone didn’t want this guy identified,” Vaughn continued. “They were removed after he died. He died from a stab wound, although from the location and angle it wouldn’t have been instantaneous. It would have taken a minute or two. I’d say he’s been dead a couple of days, but I’ll have a more accurate estimate after I get him back to the lab.”

Mark stared down at the body for a few more seconds. “Is there any chance you can tell what this guy’s hair color was?”

"Judging by the color of the hair on his arms and chest, I'd say light, probably blond. Why?"

Mark exchanged a quick look with Liam. "You thinking what I'm thinking?"

Liam nodded. "This could be the man Rebecca saw stabbed."

"Do you think she'd recognize his clothes if she saw him?" Mark asked, knowing he was grasping at straws.

"We won't know unless we try," Liam said. "I can call her," he added quickly.

Mark barely managed to suppress a smirk. He had a feeling Liam had been just waiting for an excuse to talk to the tea shop owner.

Liam pulled out his phone and Mark noticed that his partner had programmed the woman's number into his phone already. Liam called and a moment later he was talking. "Rebecca? Hi, this is Detect- Yes, Liam, that's right," he said.

Clearly she had been waiting for him to call.

"I'm good and you? Glad to hear it. Listen, we found a body and we were wondering if you think you could identify the victim you saw based on his clothes... I'd love to have you try."

Liam walked a few feet away as he continued talking. Mark squatted down to take a closer look at the body which Vaughn was still looking over.

"I wonder why someone didn't want this guy identified," Mark mused.

"It seems kind of pointless. Whoever he is someone will report him missing if they haven't already. It's not like this is the big city where people can vanish and no one notices."

There was a trace of bitterness in Vaughn's voice that caught Mark's attention. It sounded like there was a story there. He wanted to ask, but he didn't. Everyone was entitled to what little privacy they could get in this world where every little thing was over-scrutinized. If Vaughn wanted to talk about it, he would.

"Maybe the killer only needed him to go unidentified for a short period of time. Maybe he knew that for some reason people didn't expect this guy to be in contact for a few days," Mark said, thinking out loud.

"Like what, he was supposed to be on vacation or a business trip?"

"Could be something like that," Mark mused. "Or it's possible he's not from around here in which case it could take weeks to identify him."

"That's true. Lots of tourists and business travelers come to southern California each year. Some of them even make it to Pine Springs."

"And some never leave," Mark said.

He stood as Liam ended his call and headed back over. "Well?"

"She'll try. Only problem is, she can't come down to the morgue later so she's headed here now."

Mark grimaced. It was less than ideal, but they needed all the information they could get as fast as they could get it. Something in his gut told him if it took too long to identify the victim, the killer would be long gone by the time they figured out where to start looking.

Rebecca arrived in less than fifteen minutes and the tea shop owner was soon standing next to Liam, staring down at the body.

"I guess it doesn't really matter that I couldn't see his face," she said after a few moments.

"As it turns out, no. Do the clothes look familiar?" Mark asked.

She nodded. "That's what the victim was wearing. The stab wound is in the right place, too. I'd be willing to say that this is him."

"Any idea why the killer might have wanted to obscure his identity?" Liam asked.

"No. That's very strange. Seems more like a mafia, terrorist, serial killer sort of move and not just a standard murder."

"Well now that we think we've found the victim to the murder you witnessed, hopefully we can figure out who he was soon so we can try and find the killer," Mark said.

"At least now I know you believe me," Rebecca said.

"I don't think anyone will doubt you ever again," Liam said.

Mark raised an eyebrow, but didn't say anything.

"Is there anything else I can help with?" she asked.

"Not at the moment," Mark told her.

"Okay. I'll get going then. It's going to be a busy day. I have three birthday tea parties booked."

"Good luck with them," Liam said. "Here, I can walk you to your car."

"I think he likes her," Vaughn commented when the two were out of earshot.

"Brilliant police work on that one," Mark said sarcastically.

Vaughn grinned. "I'm just about done here. Is there anything else you need to see?"

“No, I think we’re good for now. Thanks, though,” Mark said.

He turned and headed to their car which was parked in front of Rebecca’s. She waved goodbye to Liam and pulled into the street just as Mark walked up. Liam stared intently after her.

“Should I remind you of the code of conduct?” Mark asked.

“She’s not a suspect, she’s a witness,” Liam snapped as he turned to face Mark.

Mark took a step back and held his hands up at shoulder height. “Take it easy, I was teasing,” he said. He was surprised to have elicited such a strong reaction from his normally even-tempered partner.

“I’m sorry, that was uncalled for,” Liam said looking suddenly sheepish.

“It’s okay. Everyone’s entitled to feel strongly about things and express it. I’m just not used to seeing you do it. Of course you’re right, she’s fair game because she’s not a suspect.”

Liam sighed and frowned, turning to stare in the direction that Rebecca had gone.

“What’s wrong?”

“I keep wondering if maybe she should be,” Liam muttered, almost too softly for Mark to hear him.

“What do you mean?” Mark asked, trying to smile even though Liam’s words chilled him.

“She was active duty military. She served in a war zone. It’s not like she’s not capable of doing this,” Liam said, gesturing to the body.

Mark stared at him in shock. “Are you serious?”

Liam shrugged. “I don’t know, maybe.”

"And what? She called claiming to have witnessed a murder in order to throw suspicion off of herself?"

"It's not like it's never been done before."

"You have a very suspicious mind."

"I wish I didn't," Liam admitted.

"You know, if you want to investigate her, we can."

"I don't *want* to investigate her."

"Sorry, poor choice of words. If you think we should be looking into her, we can."

"I don't know. Maybe I'm just being paranoid."

Mark clapped a hand on his partner's shoulder. "In Pine Springs, there's no such thing. We'll check her out and then we can all rest easy."

At least, he hoped so.

~

Cindy was completely on edge as she took her seat in the jury box. The police had spent half an hour checking every room on the floor for Wyatt before hurrying them all down to the waiting cars in the parking garage. Now Carson was sitting in the chair Wyatt had been occupying the day before. Everything just felt wrong to her.

She kept going over it in her mind, but she couldn't figure out how Wyatt could have snuck out of the hotel without the police seeing and catching him. Once he had, where would he have gone? Surely he knew that he was going to be in trouble so heading home didn't exactly seem like a smart move.

The man had been desperate to get the trial over with quickly. No one wanted to be there, but he'd been borderline hysterical about it a couple of times and she couldn't help but wonder why.

At least there had been no accidents on the way to the courthouse this morning. The only excitement after they left their hotel was when the scanners caught the fact that Carson had a phone and the bailiff confiscated it from him. He had been livid, but the rules were the rules. In all the craziness the day before they'd never sent the jurors through the metal detector. Cindy was a little sad he had lost his phone because she had been counting on being able to get to it if there was an emergency.

The trial resumed and she had to mentally shake herself to try and shift her focus from the missing juror and the confiscated phone to Jason Todd and his dead wife, Cassidy. A police officer, a well-muscled man with blond hair, was being sworn in and after taking the oath he settled into the chair and the prosecuting attorney approached him.

"Officer Nichols can you tell us what happened on the evening of August ninth of last year?"

"Yes, we had a report of a domestic disturbance with shots fired at 14 Goldfinch Lane at approximately half past seven in the evening."

"Who called in the report?"

"A neighbor who was out jogging, Mrs. Miller. She identified herself in the 911 call."

"What happened when you arrived at 14 Goldfinch Lane?"

"My partner and I were the first on the scene. We went up to the front door, rang the bell, and knocked loudly, identifying ourselves as police officers. Everything was quiet. We couldn't hear any movement or talking inside. We then proceeded to walk down the side of the house closest to Mrs. Miller's house. The blinds were raised partway in the living room and when we looked through the window we could see a very large pool of blood on the tile."

"How large?"

"Large enough to indicate that if it had come from a person that person was dead from blood loss if nothing else."

"I see. Then what did you do?" the prosecutor asked.

"Based on that and the 911 call we made the decision to enter the house forcefully. We did and we searched it from top to bottom but there was no one there."

"What did you find?"

"In addition to the pool of blood there was more blood leading to the garage. Also, there was a gun on the floor of the living room, half underneath a sofa. It had been recently fired."

"Did you determine the gun's owner?"

"Yes, it was registered to Jason Todd."

Around her Cindy could hear murmurs from some of the other jurors. The gun being registered to him wasn't particularly damning evidence, though. Lots of people owned guns. She knew a couple of them. It didn't mean he had been the one to actually fire the gun.

She was struggling to keep an open mind and to be impartial despite her instincts about the man. Over and over she kept telling herself that just because he was evil didn't mean he was guilty of this particular crime. That's all she was there to judge.

"What happened next?"

"Once we had determined that there was no one in the home we called in what we had found so that the department could send out a forensics analyst and a detective. They arrived within the hour. The forensics analyst confirmed our initial assessment that there was enough blood on the floor to confirm that someone had died there. The detectives looked around and went to question Mrs. Miller."

"And what did you and your partner do?"

"We had finished our initial search of the perimeter of the house. That was when Jason Todd came home. He drove up in his black Mercedes and demanded to know what we were doing there. After checking his identification to confirm his identity we informed him that there had been an incident in his home and that we would need to search his car."

"What did that search reveal?"

"There was some blood and several hairs in his trunk which was otherwise empty. He claimed to have no knowledge of how either could have ended up there."

"Then what happened?"

"The detectives returned from questioning Mrs. Miller. We then took Jason Todd into custody on suspicion that he had murdered his wife."

It seemed very neat and convenient, Cindy thought. Then again sometimes things were that simple. She listened as the prosecutor asked some more questions before wrapping up. It was then the defense attorney's turn to step up and ask some questions of his own.

"Doesn't it strike you as odd that my client, an intelligent man, would leave the blinds open in his living room after killing his wife?" the defense attorney asked.

"It has been my observation that many people in stressful circumstances don't think through all the details very well and often overlook things that would be obvious to them if they were calm."

"How did my client seem to you when he arrived at his home?"

"Agitated, anxious."

"Are these, in your experience, normal emotions expressed by people when dealing with police officers regardless of the circumstances?"

"Yes," Officer Nichols said, beginning to scowl.

"Did he try to run or resist arrest in any way?"

"No."

"Was he combative?"

"No."

"Did he tell you where he had been?"

"He said that he'd been working late and was just then returning home after having been gone all day."

"I have one very crucial question for you officer."

"Okay."

The defense attorney looked over at the jury box and Cindy believed he was watching them for their reactions.

"Has Cassidy Todd's body ever been found?"

"No, sir, it has not."

12

Cindy heard more murmuring around her. Like her, several of the other jurors hadn't followed the story closely or even at all, so this was a surprise to a few of them.

The defense attorney continued, clearly trying to drive the point home. "So, no body was found in the course of your investigation?"

"We did receive an anonymous tip and when we followed up on it the body of a female was found. Her head and hands were missing making identification difficult. However, the coroner was able to determine that it was not the body of Cassidy Todd."

"So, that body that reporters were going on about for weeks turned out to be unrelated to this case?"

"That is correct. The unidentified female was determined not to be Cassidy Todd."

Unidentified female. The words seemed so cold, so tragic. Cindy couldn't help but wonder if the identity of the woman had ever been discovered. She hoped so for the sake of the woman's family and friends who deserved to know what had happened to her. She couldn't imagine if someone in her life went missing and she had to forever wonder what had happened to them, if they were alive or dead. She shuddered at the thought even as she found herself saying a prayer for the unknown woman's family.

~

Normally Jeremiah had Thursdays off. With Marie out, though, he was in the office answering calls and handling the business that had to get done before Shabbat. It was nearly lunchtime when Jeremiah's cell rang. He glanced at it and saw that the incoming number was from Marie's home. He hadn't known if he should be expecting a call regarding a funeral for her brother or if Isaac had a rabbi that was going to be taking care of everything.

"Hello?"

"Hello, Rabbi. This is Eric."

Jeremiah frowned, somewhat surprised that Marie's husband was calling. In the background he could hear what sounded like a woman shouting.

"Eric, is everything alright?"

"No, not really. That's why I'm calling. Could you come over. Like now?"

"Sure. I can close the office for lunch."

Jeremiah heard what sounded like breaking glass.

"It might take a bit longer than that," Eric said.

"Understood. I'll be there in fifteen minutes."

"Thanks. And hurry."

Before Jeremiah could say anything else Eric had hung up. Whatever it was sounded urgent. He turned off the computer and quickly locked up. He put a sign on the door letting anyone who stopped by know that the office would reopen in the morning.

He made it to Marie and Eric's house and pulled up outside. As he got out of his car he could hear Marie shouting angrily. At least, he thought it was her. He had incurred her wrath several times over the years but he'd never heard anything like this.

He got up to the door but before he could ring the doorbell it flew open. Eric was standing there with a mixture of panic and relief on his features. "Rabbi, thank G-d you're here," he said.

"What's going on? Are the kids alright?"

"Yes, my cousin picked up Erica and Greta earlier this morning. Josiah is with his grandmother."

"That's a relief. Now suppose you tell me what the problem is?"

"Yes, of course, come in."

Jeremiah hesitantly followed Eric inside the house. Once Eric had closed the door the man leaned against it as though to say that there was no way he was letting Jeremiah leave. It spoke volumes about Eric's mental state and his hope that Jeremiah could fix whatever was so desperately wrong.

"The coroner won't release Isaac's body today so that we can get him buried before Shabbat. Neither has he allowed a Shomer to be present."

Jeremiah winced, knowing that was partly his fault. The coroner wouldn't have to be taking such time with the body had it not been for Jeremiah suggesting to Mark that foul play might have been the cause of Isaac's apparent heart attack. In Jewish tradition it was important to bury the body as soon as possible and Marie and her family would not want to have to wait until Sunday or even later to take care of it.

A Shomer, also known as a watchman, was supposed to stay with the body at all times from death to burial because the deceased was not supposed to be left alone. Family members usually handled that although someone outside of the family could be hired to do it if necessary. Jeremiah understood the coroner not wanting people underfoot or accidentally contaminating evidence, but he'd have to see what he could do. Maybe there were a couple of police officers willing to help out in that regard. He made a mental note to talk to Mark about it.

Another shout came from deeper within the house followed by something else breaking. Eric winced.

"Would you believe that my cousin is a doctor and already gave her a sedative?" he asked.

"She's clearly very upset," Jeremiah responded. "I never even knew she had a brother until I found out what had happened to him."

"Very few did. I think that's part of what's making this so hard. They were estranged, to put it lightly."

"I'm very sorry to hear that."

"Yeah."

There was another crash.

"I'm going to go talk to her," Jeremiah said.

"Thank you," Eric said. "Maybe she'll listen to you."

From the sounds coming from the other room Jeremiah doubted that Marie was in the mood to listen to anyone right then. Still, he had to try.

"She's in the kitchen," Eric said.

Jeremiah nodded and headed for the kitchen, hoping Marie didn't break any more glassware before he could talk to her.

She was leaning against one of the counters, face swollen. She looked up in surprise as he walked in.

"Rabbi, what are you doing here?" she asked a bit incredulously.

"Eric asked me to come," he said. "He told me what's happening."

"It's an abomination. He won't release the body," she said, her voice shaking.

"Marie. I understand how you feel." He took a deep breath. "But you suggested to me that I look into this, see if your brother was murdered. Unfortunately that takes time. The coroner can't release the body until he's done a very thorough examination and ruled out anything but death by natural causes. That can take a while, especially if he has to run toxicology reports." He said it as gently as he could. No one wanted to picture their loved one being tested and cut into after they had died. If she wanted answers, peace of mind, this was what had to be.

Tears filled her eyes. Slowly, as though her legs just couldn't support her anymore, she slid onto the floor. Once there she tucked her knees up to her chest and wrapped her arms around her legs.

"I know I asked you to find out...I just didn't think...I didn't know it would take so long."

Jeremiah sat down on the floor so he could be on the same level as her. "I know, but it's going to be okay. Isaac would understand. He was a reporter, getting answers was his life's work. He'd want you to be sure."

Marie shook her head. "I doubt he'd want to give me any peace of mind. He wouldn't even talk to me."

And there it was, the sudden flash of anger, bitterness, and regret in her voice. The shouting and breaking things wasn't about having to delay the funeral. It was about the fact that they'd never reconciled.

"What happened between you two?" he asked quietly.

She took a deep breath, shuddering as she did so.

"We were very close growing up even though he was four years older than I was. We were raised Orthodox. Our parents were pretty strict."

"I didn't know."

She nodded. "Don't get me wrong, I love G-d, I love my faith, but Orthodox isn't easy on a kid."

"Especially not in southern California in the eighties, I'm imagining," he said.

"Yeah. Isaac and I understood each other and we swore that we would do things a little different."

"And?"

"And he decided to do things a lot different. Freshman year of college he met a girl, fell in love, and got married. She was a Christian. My parents were furious; they disowned him. He abandoned his faith and then he abandoned me, left me alone with their bitterness, their mistrust, and I was fourteen. They became even more strict, telling me who I could be friends with and who I couldn't, what books I could read, everything."

"I'm sorry," he said softly.

Everything about Marie was becoming so much clearer, especially her seeming dislike for those she called Gentiles and her very real dislike of Cindy. To her Jeremiah and Cindy must seem like Isaac and his wife all over again.

"Initially my parents were thrilled with Eric. He came from an Orthodox home, too. But, like me, he didn't want to put all of that on his children. They were furious when we started going to a synagogue that wasn't Orthodox. They refused to speak to me for a year."

"That's harsh."

"They thought I'd lost my faith, that I was just going to be a cultural Jew and not a religious one. I told them I could never lose my faith, but they wouldn't listen. Then they finally relented a bit. I guess the thought of being estranged from both their children was too much for them."

Jeremiah couldn't help but think of his own family back in Israel, of the lost relationships because they couldn't accept him or Cindy. His heart ached for Marie.

"Then, a few years ago, Isaac's wife was killed in a car accident. I tried reaching out to him, but he rebuffed me. I shouldn't have let it go. I should have tried again."

"We always think we're going to have more time," Jeremiah said softly. "At least you did try."

She nodded. "I told him back then that I loved him."

"Then you did the best you could and you need to let it go," he said.

"I know, it's just...hard...you know? And now I'm going to have to deal with my parents for the next few weeks more than I usually care to."

"They'll be grieving, like you, and perhaps that will bring you all closer together, or at least allow you the grace to deal with each other while you must."

"That would be nice. This whole experience is going to be strange. This is the first major death that my children will experience and yet they didn't even know their uncle."

"Then you must tell them all you can about him."

She nodded. "I will."

"Did he have any children?"

"No. And from what I understand he didn't go to a church...at least, not after his wife died. So we'll be the ones burying him. I would appreciate it if you would oversee it."

"I will."

"Thank you."

She was looking far calmer and starting to slur her words a little bit. Jeremiah wasn't sure if the sedative she'd been given was taking effect or if this was sheer exhaustion setting in. Either way it would probably be a good time for him to go.

Before he could move, Eric tiptoed hesitantly into the kitchen. "Everyone alright?" he asked, worry heavy in his voice.

"Fine," Marie said, slurring even more.

"I think she should get some rest," Jeremiah said as he stood up.

"I'll get her into bed," Eric said. "Thank you so much for your help."

"You're welcome. She just needed to talk things out," Jeremiah said.

"Well, I'm glad she could with someone. She wasn't really in a talkative mood earlier."

"Don't take it badly," Jeremiah told him, putting a hand on his shoulder and willing the other man to be calm.

"I'm not. I don't care who she talked to as long as she got it out."

"You're a good man, Eric. I'll call as soon as I know anything. Please do the same."

"I will," he promised.

Three minutes later Jeremiah was in his car calling Mark.

"Yeah?" the detective asked as he answered the phone.

"Things going that well?" Jeremiah asked.

Mark grunted. "More chaos and uncertainty than I like."

"What's going on?"

"Found a dead body, could be the guy who was reported stabbed a couple of days ago, could be someone else."

"Okay."

"But the most exciting news of the morning was that one of the jurors seems to have pulled a Houdini."

"I don't follow."

"The man disappeared from his hotel room last night. Vanished without a trace."

"How did he slip past the guards?"

"That's what all of us would like to know. Care to shed any light on that particular problem?"

"Not particularly."

"Come on, Rabbi, I know you're just waiting for me to look the other way for five minutes so you can break into the hotel and see Cindy."

"If you say so," Jeremiah said warily.

"Please, I know it, my wife knows it, all your friends know it. Heck half of Pine Springs probably knows it."

"And?"

"And I'd like you to tell me how you would do it. Or, better yet, how you'd get back out again without getting caught."

"Are you inviting me to the crime scene?" Jeremiah asked.

"Officially I'm not inviting you anywhere. And it's not a crime scene. At least, I hope it isn't. I just want to know how someone escapes that building without our knowing it."

"I can't give away all my trade secrets," Jeremiah said.

"Come on, if someone can get out then someone can get in. Which means someone can get to Cindy."

"That is what they call a low blow."

"Yes, yes it is. I'm not proud of it, but hey, if it protects people I'd do it again."

"The missing juror, did he take his things with him?"

"Yes."

"So, he had to smuggle luggage as well as himself?"

"Yes, making it all the more unfathomable how he pulled that off."

If he did pull it off, Jeremiah thought. Out loud he said, "I actually need a favor from you."

"What is it?"

"The coroner won't release Isaac's body to his family for burial yet. Now, I understand why, but it's Jewish custom that someone sit with the deceased until they're buried."

"There's no way that the coroner's going to let me put a civilian in there around the clock."

"Obviously, but if there was someone who wasn't a civilian necessarily who could sit with the body."

There was a pause and then Mark asked, "Do they have to be Jewish?"

"It would be preferable."

"I'll see what I can do," Mark said with a heavy sigh. "In the meantime please think about telling me how the guy could have left the hotel."

"Which juror was it?" Jeremiah asked, wondering if it was the same one who had been talking to Isaac the day before.

"Name's Wyatt. From all reports he was real anxious to get jury duty over with."

"What happens to the trial with him missing?"

"Nothing. They just moved one of the alternates to his seat."

"What's his name?"

"Um, Carson, I believe."

Also not Tanner. Jeremiah had been hoping he could connect the man with Wyatt in some way, but it didn't look like that was going to happen.

~

Mark hung up the phone with Jeremiah feeling frustrated. He rubbed his forehead for a moment. He could feel a headache coming on. There really was too much going on this week and he had this terrible feeling that he had so many balls up in the air that sooner or later one or more of them were going to drop.

"Everything okay?" Liam asked.

"Oh sure. I just have to find a couple of Jewish police personnel willing to give up their off time to babysit a corpse."

"Okay, that sounds...weird."

"Don't I know it," Mark said with a groan. "Sometimes the rabbi can be high maintenance."

"But worth it, though. Look at the number of cases he's helped solve, criminals he's stopped."

"Yeah, I know, the guy's a frickin' hero. I just wish that, I don't know..."

"That you could get him to do as you ask?"

"Yeah, exactly! Would it be so hard, really, to let me call the shots every once in a while?"

"For him it would probably be next to impossible," Liam said. "A guy like that's not so good at taking orders."

"Tell me about it."

~

The afternoon seemed to drag by and Cindy began to believe she'd been sitting in her juror's chair for four days instead of four hours. She glanced up and down and saw the same bleary-eyed looks on several other faces. Tanner, of course, was a notable exception. He was perched on the edge of his seat, leaning forward, rapturously transfixed by the testimony from a female witness who claimed to have had an affair with Jason Todd and said that his marriage had been in ruins when she met him.

Cindy barely managed to stifle a yawn. Just in time the judge wound things down. She also had to use the restroom fairly badly since one of the other female jurors had managed to flood the one they had access to at the beginning of lunch. She thought about asking the bailiff to escort her to another one, but decided that she could hold it for the short ride back to the hotel.

When the car she was in hit the fifth red light in a row she was deeply regretting her decision as she squirmed in her seat and crossed her legs. At long last she was in the elevator heading up to their floor in the hotel.

The elevator doors opened and she turned toward her room, walking as quickly as she could. She heard the phone ring in the common area and seconds later a police officer called, "Cindy, telephone, it's a Jeremiah."

"Tell him I'll call him back," she tossed over her shoulder as she made it into the corridor. Seconds later she was outside her room. She unlocked it, stepped inside, and screamed as a dark figure loomed in front of her.

13

A hand clamped down on Cindy's mouth and someone made a frantic shushing sound. It took her a second to realize that it was Jeremiah. She instantly stopped struggling and threw her arms around his neck. He moved his hand and she kissed him.

"Sorry, I tried calling the phone out there to tell you not to be startled," he said.

She heard footsteps running in the hall and a moment later there was a pounding on her door.

"Miss, are you alright?"

Jeremiah stepped into the bathroom and shut the door and Cindy opened the door to the room a crack. "Yes, sorry. I saw a spider. I managed to kill it by myself, though, my fiancé would be so proud," she told the police officer who was standing there.

"A spider?"

"Yes, they scare me terribly. And I wasn't expecting to see one. I'm okay, though, thank you for checking on me." She gave him what she hoped was a reassuring smile before closing the door in his face.

Jeremiah opened the bathroom door and put his finger to his lips. He listened at the door for a moment and then nodded, seemingly satisfied that the officer had returned to his post.

"I have to go to the bathroom," Cindy whispered.

He nodded and got out of her way, heading to the far side of her room where the table and chairs were. Cindy dashed into the bathroom and emerged a couple minutes later feeling much better.

"Should I go and make my return call to you since I told the officer I would?" she asked.

He nodded. "Just to be on the safe side. It will help allay any suspicions he has, too, about what made you scream."

"So he doesn't come back to see if a strange man broke into my room?" she teased.

"Or if a familiar face is hiding out here," he said.

She frowned. "Are you talking about Wyatt?"

"Yes."

"You heard about him disappearing?"

"I did, and we can talk about it when you get back from calling me."

"Okay," she said, nodding her head.

She exited the room, being sure to close the door firmly behind her. She strode confidently toward the common area and made for the phone.

"You said Jeremiah was calling, right?" she asked, hoping her voice was calm.

"Yes. I told him you'd call him back. Are you sure you're okay?" he asked.

"Fine. I killed it with my shoe and then flushed the body down the toilet. Thanks for coming to check on me, though. If I see another spider I might lose my nerve and have to call you to come get it."

The officer smiled. “My wife is the same way so I’m used to it. Call if you need me.”

“Thank you.”

She sat down in the chair next to the phone and then called Jeremiah. When he picked up she said, “Hi, honey, how was your day?”

“Not bad and yours?”

“A bit boring until a few minutes ago. You’ll never guess what I did. I killed a spider by myself.”

“Oh good, I never have to worry about you and spiders again.”

“Think again, mister. I still need you to kill the nasty little things when they poke their heads up.”

“Don’t I do that with all nasty things that get near you?” he asked in a flirtatious tone.

She felt herself blushing. “I miss you.”

“I miss you, too.”

She looked up and saw Tanner heading her way. He stopped a few feet from her and it was clear that he wanted to use the phone.

“Well, I have to go, someone else needs the phone,” she said, appreciative of the excuse to cut the call short. “I love you.”

“Love you, too. Get back here and I’ll show you how much,” he said.

She was grinning from ear to ear as she hung up the phone. “All yours,” she told Tanner a little breathlessly as she headed back toward her room.

As soon as she made it inside Jeremiah pounced again, but this time he covered her mouth with kisses and held her tight. When he finally let her go she felt a little dizzy and breathless. "Remind me to get sequestered more often," she said.

"I missed you so much," he told her, brushing a strand of hair out of her face.

"I missed you, too."

He pulled her into the room and they sat down at the table holding hands. He gently rubbed the back of hers with his thumb, making the skin tingle.

"How are you? Are you okay?" he asked.

"I am now," she said, realizing she had not stopped smiling.

"You know how much I worry."

"I know, and I worry that you worry," she teased.

Talking about missing jurors and Marie's dead brother was suddenly the last thing she wanted to do, but she didn't know how long he'd be able to stay.

"I guess we should talk business," she said reluctantly.

He laughed. "By that do you mean church and synagogue business or mystery business?"

"Well we can certainly talk about the former, but I was referencing the latter," she said.

"Fair enough. The coroner is still examining Isaac, Marie's brother, to see if he might have been poisoned or something."

"Poor Marie."

"Yes, she's pretty distraught. I have nothing new on that front, though."

"And you heard that Wyatt was missing this morning?"

"Yes, Mark told me," Jeremiah said.

"The police scoured the entire floor, searched everyone's room, and they couldn't find any trace of him. It was the spookiest thing. He vanished sometime during the night and no one seems to have seen or heard anything. I'm just not sure how he did it. The police don't seem to know either."

Jeremiah frowned. "It would be very difficult for the average person to have left here without being seen by one of the police officers," he said.

"So, what are you saying, that Wyatt wasn't average? That he had experience with getting in and out of places?" Cindy asked.

"No, what I'm saying is that I don't think he actually left the building."

She blinked at him in surprise. "I told you, they searched the whole floor. Do you think he could be on a different floor?"

"No, I think he never left this floor."

"How is that possible?" Cindy asked. "All the other rooms on this floor are occupied. Is someone hiding him? If so, where that the police couldn't find him earlier? That makes no sense."

"Let's go look at his room," Jeremiah said, standing up.

"The police have already been over it."

"Yes, but they don't think in the same way that I do," he said as he headed for the door. "Which room is his?"

"It's the last one on this side, at the end of the hall," she said. "The guard will see us, though."

"Go out there, make another phone call. He'll be paying attention to you and I can get down the hall and into that other room. When you come back here, if he's not looking you can come to the other room, if not, I'll meet you back in here."

"Okay," Cindy said, taking a deep breath. She rose and crossed over to stand next to him by the door. "Good luck."

Her hand was on the door when he pulled her into his arms and kissed her. “That’s for luck,” he said with a smile after he had let go.

She wanted to leave the room now even less than before. Still, getting to the bottom of this might in some way get her home earlier. She realized it was probably a vain hope, but a girl could dream.

She headed out the door and eased it closed so that it didn’t close completely. She walked toward the lounge area across from the elevators. The police officer on duty looked up. “Another spider?” he asked.

“No, just another phone call,” she said.

He nodded and watched her for a moment before returning his attention to a book he was reading.

She passed in front of him, and then sat down in the chair next to the table with the phone. Down the hall she could see a flicker of movement.

She picked up the receiver and dialed Geanie’s cell. When Geanie answered the surprise was clear in her voice. “Hey, is everything okay?”

“Not entirely.”

“You can’t tell me more over the phone, can you?”

“Exactly,” Cindy said.

She was struggling with wanting to try to tell Geanie what was going on in a way that the police officer wouldn’t understand what she was doing. As she groped for the right words she reminded herself that this call was only supposed to be a diversion, not an actual check-in.

“I’m sure it will be fine,” Cindy said. “How’s Blackie?”

“Do you know what your baby kitty did today?” Geanie asked.

“No.”

"I caught him in the kitchen feeding candy to Clarice."

Clarice was Joseph and Geanie's poodle. "How on earth was he managing that?" Cindy asked.

"We had a candy dish on the counter filled with some hard candies. Blackie was on the counter sitting next to it and every time Clarice barked Blackie would pick up a candy with his paw and throw it down to her."

Cindy burst out laughing as she pictured it in her mind. The police officer turned and gave her a startled glance. "My friends are babysitting my cat and they caught him stealing candy for their dog," she explained to him.

He chuckled and nodded his head before turning his attention back to his book.

"I take it you put a stop to it?" Cindy asked Geanie.

"We put away the candy dish. I just can't wait to see what they're going to do next."

"If it's something cute, take a picture for me."

"I will. Is there anything we can do for you?"

"I wish there was. Just keep taking care of my baby."

"Will do."

Cindy guessed that enough time had passed so she reluctantly said goodnight and hung up. She stood slowly and began to walk back toward her side of the floor. "Goodnight," she told the officer.

"Goodnight," he said, without looking up from his book.

She walked at a normal pace until she was certain he couldn't see her out of his peripheral vision. Then she sped up and made it down the length of the hall, glancing back twice to make sure he wasn't watching.

He wasn't.

She pushed open the door to Wyatt's room which Jeremiah had left slightly ajar for her and then closed it as quietly behind her as she could.

"Good job," Jeremiah said quietly from across the room where he appeared to be inspecting the curtains. She noticed that he was wearing a pair of black gloves which he hadn't had on earlier.

"Thanks. Have you found anything?"

"Not yet," he said with a frown. "That's the weird part. This room is cleaner than yours."

"Maybe because nobody's staying in it anymore," Cindy said feeling somewhat defensive.

"No, I mean clean, like it's been wiped down professionally. No fingerprints, no trace evidence that someone was even here, let alone that they snuck out."

"Are you suggesting that someone helped him?"

"No, I'm suggesting someone killed him," Jeremiah said.

"What? Why?" Cindy asked. "I mean, that makes no sense. How could someone have killed him and gotten rid of the body and all the evidence with the police just down the hall? This floor is sealed off. The only way on or off this floor is past the police. You think they would have noticed something."

"Not if the killer was one of the other jurors. And not if he disposed of the body in the way I think he might have."

Cindy felt a chill dance down her spine when Jeremiah said the killer could be another juror.

"Why? It's not like any of us knew any of the rest of us prior to being selected to be on the jury."

"Are you certain?"

She started to say that she was, but then stopped. She realized that she couldn't actually say with one hundred percent certainty that no one there had known Wyatt before that week. He hadn't exactly seemed like the easiest person to get along with and he had wanted off the jury in a big hurry. Maybe it was because of someone else on it. She rubbed her arms, trying to get the chill that she felt to go away.

Mentally she began reviewing everyone else and trying to remember if she'd seen them interact with Wyatt, or even if she'd seen them trying to avoid Wyatt or vice versa.

"How would they have killed him and gotten rid of the evidence?" she asked, even as her mind was racing through the events of the last couple of days.

"Let's check out the bathroom," he said.

Together they entered the cramped bathroom. Cindy had no idea what it was they were hoping to find in there. Jeremiah instantly began studying the bathtub shower combination.

"Notice anything odd?" he asked her.

"The shower curtain."

It was true. Instead of hanging straight down like it should be, the shower curtain was draped up and over the curtain rod in such a way as to give several feet of clearance between the bottom of the curtain and the top of the tub. "Maybe he liked baths and really didn't want the grungy curtain in his way," she suggested.

"Someone certainly didn't want it in the way. I'm fairly confident that the killer draped it like this to keep it from being damaged and giving away what happened here."

"What did happen here?" she asked.

"If someone murdered him, they could have put the body in the bathtub, poured some caustic soda on it, and waited for it to dissolve everything but the skeleton."

"You can't be serious," she said, aghast at the thought.

He nodded. "It would take less than twenty minutes. Did the police inspect your bags when you got to the hotel that first night?"

"No."

"Then it would have been simple for him to bring the caustic soda with him, hiding it in his luggage."

"How do you know...never mind," she said, quickly rethinking her question. "The killer would still have the bones, though. What would he do with those?"

"Hide them. He could put them in a duffel bag and clear them out once this whole thing was over."

"You mean, what's left of Wyatt could be in a duffel bag in someone's room right now?"

Jeremiah shook his head slowly. "He could be, but the killer would probably want to store them somewhere else, just to be on the safe side."

"The police would have found it when they went through this room if it was here," Cindy said. Even as she spoke, though, she found her eyes drifting up to the ceiling tiles.

"We have this kind of ceiling in some of the Sunday School rooms at the church. I believe you can lift the panels up to get to a crawlspace."

"You certainly can," Jeremiah said.

He hopped up on the bathroom counter and ran his fingers over a couple of the tiles before pushing up on one of them experimentally. He peered into the crawlspace for a moment before saying, "I need a flashlight."

"Do you have a flashlight app on your phone?" Cindy asked.

"I do. Thanks for the reminder." He pulled his phone out of his pocket and he shone the light into the crawlspace.

"There's something in here," he said.

Her stomach clenched slightly. "Can you tell what it is?"

"It's a bag."

He pushed the ceiling tile up higher and then slid out a long, dark bag. After replacing the ceiling tile he got down off the counter. Cindy could feel her heart starting to race as he put the bag in the middle of the floor and then started to unzip it.

A moment later she jumped back, barely stifling a scream.

14

Cindy's muffled scream caused Jeremiah to jump. He hadn't expected her to react so strongly.

"You've seen a body before," he said.

She nodded, hand still covering her mouth. Slowly she lowered it. "I can't believe that is...was...Wyatt. And it's like the skull is staring at me."

The bag was full of bones, as he had suspected it would be. Unfortunately the skull had been directly facing Cindy when he opened the bag. He pulled out his cell phone.

Mark answered on the second ring. "Did you find a way out?" the detective asked without preamble.

"No, but I found a way in...and it turns out there's no need to find a way out."

"I'm not going to like this, am I?"

"No, but it will help you out with some unanswered questions."

"Like what?"

"Like what happened to your missing juror."

"You found him?"

"I think so."

"You think so?" Mark echoed.

"I can't really identify him off what I have in front of me, but I'm reasonably certain it's him."

He expected Mark to swear under his breath, but instead the other man just sighed heavily. “Okay, where are you?”

“In his room at the hotel.”

That elicited an expletive from the detective. A moment later he said, “Don’t move until I get there. Don’t do anything else or talk to anyone.”

“We won’t,” Jeremiah promised.

“*We*. I should have figured. Where one of you is and there’s trouble, the other one can never be far behind. I’ll be there in fifteen minutes.”

Jeremiah hung up and glanced at Cindy who was staring fixedly at the skull. He touched her shoulder and she jumped.

“Why don’t we go wait for Mark in the other room?” he suggested.

She nodded. “Good idea.”

They moved back into the bedroom and both sat down on the foot of the bed. He could tell Cindy was still agitated so he put his arm around her shoulders and gave them a squeeze.

“It’s going to be okay.”

She gave him a wan smile. “You think it’s going to be this way for the rest of our lives?”

“What way?”

“Us, solving mysteries.”

“I don’t know,” he confessed. “We certainly seem to find more than our share of them, that’s for certain. What I do know is that whatever comes, we’ll be together.”

She nodded, her smile growing larger.

They sat there in silence for a few minutes before finally hearing a sound at the door. They stood up just as Mark and Liam entered followed by a third man who

Jeremiah recognized from other crime scenes. Jeremiah was pretty sure he worked forensics. They closed the door behind them.

Liam whistled low as he glanced into the bathroom.

"Can you show me exactly where you found this?" the forensics guy asked.

Jeremiah stepped forward and pointed up to the tile he had moved. "I lifted that one and the bag was over there," he said, pointing to roughly where it had been in the crawlspace.

The man put on a pair of gloves, grabbed a flashlight, and got up onto the counter.

"Let's give him some space," Mark said.

Jeremiah nodded and headed back into the bedroom and again sat down on the edge of the bed.

Mark glanced pointedly at Jeremiah's hands. "Nice gloves. Planning for a little breaking and entering tonight?" he asked, sarcasm dusting his voice.

Jeremiah shrugged. "You know what they say, it's good to be prepared."

Mark rolled his eyes and turned to Cindy. "Okay, what happened?"

"Jeremiah came to check-in on me and make sure I was okay."

"Something I believe several of us had told him *not* to do," Mark said, sighing in obvious frustration.

"And then you practically begged me to earlier today," Jeremiah said, narrowing his eyes in a glare.

"Fair enough," Mark said. "Can you blame me? It's getting crazy around here. I was hoping you'd just scout the place out, though, and not actually break in."

"Like that was going to happen," Liam burst out.

"Given the circumstances, how could you expect him not to check in and make sure things were okay?" Cindy said, a touch of anger in her voice.

"Okay, and I pretty much asked for it, so moving on," Mark said. "Okay, he came to visit. Then what?"

"We discussed the missing juror and how odd it was that he could manage to leave the floor unnoticed. At which point Jeremiah suggested that maybe he hadn't left at all."

Mark looked at Jeremiah.

He shrugged. "It seemed like a more obvious explanation than him being able to sneak out unobserved."

"Despite the fact that you yourself had just snuck in unobserved?"

"I was, of course, assuming that he didn't share my background or skill set," Jeremiah said.

"Because pretty much no one does. Okay, that does make sense," Mark said.

"So, we decided to investigate ourselves," Cindy said.

"Even though you already knew there was no sign of him in his room?" Mark asked.

"Of course. We were thinking there might have been something that was overlooked. So, when we got into the room-"

"How did you pull that off without being seen, by the way?" Liam interrupted.

"Trade secret," Jeremiah said.

Mark took a deep breath. "I'm going to let that go for the moment. So, you're in the room. What next?"

"Jeremiah pointed out that it was too clean. There weren't even fingerprints. That made us even more suspicious. Then when we checked the bathroom the odd way that the shower curtain was draped caught our attention. Jeremiah theorized that someone could have snuck into the room, killed Wyatt, and then used caustic soda to destroy everything but the bones."

Mark turned to Jeremiah, a strange look on his face. He started to speak and Jeremiah shook his head. "You don't want to know."

"You're right," Mark said quickly, turning his attention back to Cindy.

"We have those same sort of ceiling tiles that are here in the bathroom in a few of the rooms at church so I knew there was likely a crawlspace up there. Jeremiah got up on the counter, pushed back one of the tiles, and found the bag with the bones."

"If they turn out to belong to Wyatt that would certainly explain why no one saw him leave the hotel," Mark said. "Of course, now we have the question of how did someone get in to kill him and then get out without being noticed." He looked at Jeremiah. "After all, it would take someone with a very special skill set to pull that off."

Jeremiah cleared his throat. "We have a simpler explanation."

"Oh good," Mark said.

"One of the other jurors killed him," Cindy said.

"Oh, bad. Very, very bad," Mark said.

"I can start digging into his background more, figure out who might have had a reason to want him dead," Liam said.

Mark nodded. "Did you notice anyone acting like they knew him?"

Cindy shook her head. "No."

"This complicates everything," Mark said. "A juror skipping out is one thing. A juror murdered, and potentially by another juror, is an entirely different matter."

"Sounds like adequate grounds for a mistrial," Jeremiah said, hoping that this meant that Cindy could go home and put all this behind her.

"We're not doing anything rash just yet," Mark said. "That's part of the reason just the three of us showed up here tonight. If the killer is another juror and a mistrial is declared and everyone is sent home, the killer could run and we wouldn't have a chance to catch him. No, as long as the trial continues we'll have all of them under our control."

"You can't be serious," Jeremiah said. "You're putting the lives of all the others in jeopardy," he said, feeling anger beginning to rise in him.

"Not necessarily. We don't even know what the motive for killing Wyatt was. It's possible it had nothing to do with the trial itself."

"If that was the case, though, why kill him here? Why not do it last week or two weeks from now? Why risk killing him right under the nose of the police?"

"It could have been spontaneous, a crime of passion or something," Liam suggested.

Jeremiah turned and glared at Mark's partner. "The killer used industrial chemicals to remove the flesh from the body. That's not the sort of thing room service can just send up. He had to have brought it with him on check-in. So, this was planned before arrival here at the hotel."

He forced himself to take a deep breath. Liam was a good guy and a good detective. It wasn't his fault that he was having to play catch-up on this whole situation.

“While it could have been any of the jurors, it would have been easier for one of the ones on this side of the building to do it,” Cindy pointed out. “Otherwise the killer would have had to walk by the officer on duty carrying a duffel and heading for the other side of the building. You’d think that would have been noticed.”

“You would think, but I’m not ruling out the possibility that whoever the killer was that they didn’t have some level of skill or experience. I mean, someone willing to dissolve a body and hide the bones in the ceiling doesn’t strike me as a first-time killer,” Mark said.

“Unless they were very thorough and did their research ahead of time,” Jeremiah pointed out. “Even an amateur can figure out how to do just about anything these days if they know where to go to get the information.”

“I’m getting a headache,” Mark declared.

“Hopefully by doing some digging we can connect Wyatt with someone here,” Liam said.

Jeremiah seriously doubted that. He had a feeling that whoever had killed Wyatt had not known him personally, but rather had been hired to do some sort of job. And he still wasn’t convinced that this had nothing to do with the trial. A business rival or an angry ex could have had him killed at any time. Unless, of course, they really needed an airtight alibi for themselves when it happened.

Unlike Jason Todd did when it came to the murder of his wife. That’s the whole reason we’re all here in the first place, Jeremiah thought.

“Can’t you just search people’s rooms?” Cindy asked. “The caustic soda isn’t here. Whoever has it is probably the killer.”

Before anyone could respond the forensics expert called from the bathroom, "Detectives, you're going to want to see this."

Moments later they were all four staring at the man as he stood on the countertop, carefully holding a bottle in his gloved hand.

"I believe this is the chemical in question. It was up there as well," he said, pointing to the ceiling.

Mark sighed. "It was a nice thought, Cindy, but we're going to have to find the killer some other way."

"Be careful with that stuff," Jeremiah cautioned.

"You don't have to tell me," the man said as he cautiously climbed down off the counter. "I've seen what stuff like this can do."

Jeremiah put an arm around Cindy and steered her back into the bedroom. He didn't want her anywhere near that kind of chemical. It only took Mark and Liam a few seconds to join them.

"The first step, obviously, is to see if those bones actually are the remains of Wyatt. Hopefully we can match the dental records," Mark said. "If they're not then things get to be even more complicated than they already are."

"How do you intend to flush out the killer?" Jeremiah asked.

"I don't know yet. I just know we need to keep this absolutely quiet. You can't tell anyone what you found or even that the police suspect that Wyatt didn't leave of his own free will," Mark said.

"Okay," Cindy said. "No one will hear anything from me."

"I'm counting on it. Man, I knew this Jason Todd trial was going to be trouble, but I had no idea. Three bodies.

One dead body with no hands and a head and a witness that can't identify him or the killer. One dead reporter who may or may not have had a heart attack. And now one dead juror with no flesh at all."

"You're forgetting a missing body," Cindy said.

Mark turned to look at her. "Whose?"

"Cassidy Todd."

Cindy glanced from Mark to Jeremiah. "Apparently her body has never been found. The body of the woman they did find that they thought might be her wasn't. She had her head and hands removed, too, but the coroner was still able to confirm that it wasn't Cassidy."

Cindy's eyes suddenly opened wide and she turned back to Mark. "What did you say about a body you found this week with no head and no hands?"

Mark frowned. "On Sunday a woman witnessed a murder but by the time officers arrived both the killer and the victim were gone. Trace evidence at the scene did point to a crime. This morning a body was found in a vacant lot missing the head and hands. The clothes were similar to what the victim was wearing, but we have no way to identify him yet."

"Just like the woman who wasn't Cassidy. Could they be related?"

Mark shook his head. "It's an old trick to obscure identification. It's weird but there's no connection between the two."

"You actually don't know that since you don't know who the man was," Jeremiah said.

"I'm not even sure whether they figured out who the woman was. The same person could have killed them both," Cindy said.

Mark crossed to a chair and sat down heavily, running his fingers through his hair. "This week just keeps getting weirder and weirder," he muttered.

"This is interesting, but it's all circumstantial," Liam said. "I mean, yes, they found that woman's body when they were searching for Cassidy Todd, but do we even know if she had anything to do with the Todd case?"

"They found her body from an anonymous tip that suggested it was Cassidy's body," Cindy said. "That's what they told us in the trial."

Mark looked pained. "Which you shouldn't be telling us. You shouldn't even be in this room."

"There's a killer on the loose, maybe more than one, now's not the time to quibble," Cindy said.

"Quibble!" Mark burst out then put his head in his hands.

"It's possible that she could have been completely unrelated and someone took that opportunity to reveal her whereabouts, maybe out of a guilty conscience or maybe hoping that everyone would think it was Cassidy thus letting that poor woman's real killer go free," Liam said.

"I just keep feeling in my gut that it's all connected," Cindy said. "It's just too coincidental otherwise."

"I'm happy with something being coincidental," Mark said.

"I agree with Cindy," Jeremiah said. "There's something going on here that we're not aware of yet. I don't know how it's all connected, but I can see that there is a pattern. We just need to put the puzzle pieces together."

"Yes," Cindy said. "What's our next move?"

For just a moment Mark sat there, looking completely lost. Jeremiah couldn't help but feel sorry for him. Then the detective shook his head and seemed to pull himself together.

"Okay, our next move is to get the two of you out here," he muttered. "Ideally with no one seeing."

They all moved to the door and Jeremiah edged it open quietly. Liam and Mark stepped into the hallway first and Cindy and Jeremiah walked close behind them, Jeremiah stooping slightly. They paused in the hallway in front of Cindy's room while she opened the door and then he slipped inside after her.

~

Cindy sat down on one of the chairs in her room with a yawn. Now that the adrenaline was wearing off she realized just how exhausted she was. She hadn't been sleeping well and it was finally taking its toll.

"Are you okay?" Jeremiah asked as he took a seat in the other chair.

"Yeah. I'm tired and I'm a little freaked out. I keep telling myself, though, that whoever killed Wyatt had a reason to do so and they're not just randomly going to be going after jurors."

She shuddered slightly. She hated random destruction and acts of violence. They frightened her and reminded her just how unpredictable and uncontrollable the world was. Those were things she had been doing her best to forget. Fears about that had kept her imprisoned for so many years and she couldn't return to that.

As awful as murder was, she always found it somewhat reassuring when she could find a motive behind it, a reason that one person wanted to kill another person specifically.

If another juror was the murderer, though, she was struggling to see how the attack was specific to Wyatt himself. It would have been different if it was clear that Wyatt had known one or more of the jurors before getting thrown together earlier in the week. After all, whoever had killed him had to have planned ahead. It wasn't like he had just really upset the wrong person in the last couple of days and they had flown off the handle and killed him for it.

So, how was it possible that someone here had known him and come prepared to kill him when he hadn't acted like he recognized anyone else? Maybe Wyatt had done something to someone else and a friend or relative of that person had decided to take revenge. What could that possibly be, though? Wyatt had been a bit rude and argumentative, but she had a hard time picturing him doing something that would cause someone to want to kill him.

No, the more she thought about it the more she came back to this being connected to the other two deaths that week and the poor woman that they had originally mistaken for Cassidy.

Jeremiah grabbed her hand and squeezed it. "You look worried," he said.

"I'm just hoping that whatever is happening, the killer isn't targeting other jurors," she said.

Jeremiah frowned. "We need to put an end to this. We can't endanger you this way."

"You heard what Mark said. If we don't continue on then the killer will have a chance to get away."

"Better that than to needlessly risk your life."

"So, you think the killer might be after other jurors?" she asked.

He hesitated. "I don't know. There's something going on here that's very odd. There are far easier ways to kill someone than to manage to get yourself on a jury with them. That takes a lot of resources, skill, and a bit of luck to pull something like that off."

"So, why would someone want to kill another juror if they didn't necessarily have a grudge against someone?" Cindy asked.

"To influence the outcome of a trial maybe."

"Yeah, but the trial's just started. How could anyone know how anyone else was likely to vote? Plus, now they'd be gambling on what they think the alternate might do."

"It could be about getting the alternate on as one of the main jurors where they'd have a chance to sway opinions. Who are the alternates?"

"Carson's the one who's taken Wyatt's place. There's also Lilian, who has made it very clear she doesn't want to be here."

Cindy rubbed her eyes. She really was starting to feel like she was going to pass out at any minute. Maybe it was because despite all the stress Jeremiah's presence made her feel safe and she could actually relax a bit.

"Do you want me to stay and watch over you?" he asked.

She nodded.

"Okay."

"What about Captain?"

"I dropped him off at Joseph and Geanie's earlier, just in case."

"Clever boy," she said with another yawn.

"You go get ready for bed."

Twenty minutes later Jeremiah had tucked her in and was turning out the light. "Are you going to sleep?" she asked.

"In a while. I'm going to sit up for a little bit and do some thinking."

"Okay. Love you."

"Love you, too."

She felt herself drifting off to sleep, comforted by Jeremiah's presence. Her mind was floating, and she felt warm and peaceful.

Suddenly an ear-piercing wail split the silence.

15

Cindy sat straight up with a shout of fright. "What is that?"

"Fire alarm," Jeremiah said. He was on his feet, tension in every line of his body.

"That can't be good."

"No, no it can't," he said.

"What, what do we do? You don't think there's an actual fire, do you?"

"No. I think this is another diversion, like the car."

"Then should we stay put?"

"No, the police are going to be duty bound to clear you guys off the floor and out of the hotel, just in case."

"They'll see you," Cindy said.

"Put on your shoes," he told her.

She scrambled to do as he said while the alarm kept blaring. Seconds later there was a pounding on her door. "We have to clear out!" someone that sounded like the officer on duty shouted.

"No one's going to see me," Jeremiah said. "I'm just hoping I can see whoever is behind this."

His tone was grim and she didn't know whether it was the blaring alarm or being woken up so quickly, but she was afraid. She stood up and crossed to him and grabbed his arms. "I can't lose you!" she cried.

"You're not going to lose me," he said.

"Promise me!"

"I promise. It's going to be okay. Now just get out there and do as the officers say, stick close to them."

"Okay."

She didn't want to leave him. Her heart was pounding and fear was flooding her. She kissed him and then turned, half-running for the door. At least outside she'd be away from the terrible screaming of the alarm which was in itself causing her to nearly lose it.

In the common area she was surprised to see Mark and Liam still there. Mark glanced behind her then raised an eyebrow, but didn't say anything about Jeremiah.

"Alright everyone, down the stairs," Liam boomed in a loud voice as he opened the door to the stairwell.

"Out of my way," Prudence snapped as she shoved past Cindy and a couple of others to get to the stairs. Having reached them, she bolted down them faster than Cindy could have guessed the woman could go. Even more impressive was the fact that she was doing so in heels.

Cindy and the others followed. She was surprised that as they made their way down the stairs that they weren't running into hotel guests from any of the other floors. It took her a moment to realize she didn't see doors at any of the other landings, and it finally hit her that the staircase, like the elevator, offered access only to their floor. If this was indeed a false alarm, a distraction set up by someone, she wondered if that person realized that the jurors weren't going to be mingling with the rest of the hotel guests.

There were a lot of stairs and two thirds of the way down she could feel her calf muscles begin to burn. Around her she could hear ragged gasps as some of the others struggled to catch their breath.

She stubbed her toe and lost her balance and began to tumble forward. She flailed with her arms, trying to grab onto something to keep herself from falling.

A strong hand clamped on her shoulder and pulled her back, holding her secure and then stabilizing her. She turned and saw Mike.

"Thank you," she said.

"You're welcome. You got it now?"

"Yes," she said.

"Okay."

After she moved over and was able to grab the railing to hold onto, she continued back down the stairs.

Mike stayed next to her the rest of the way down, probably thinking he might have to help her again. She was just grateful he had been there because that could have been a really terrible fall.

It was with relief that she finally made it to the bottom and out into their area of the parking garage. There several officers surrounded the group and began to lead them toward the outside.

She couldn't help but notice what everyone was wearing. Prudence was wearing a short blue negligee with her high heels. Mike was wearing sweat pants and a very baggy T-shirt. Jordan had on Superman boxer shorts and a matching T-shirt. Rachel still had the clothes on that she'd been wearing earlier as did Ezra and Tara. Like her, Joyce and Viola were wearing pajamas while Lilian had a robe wrapped around her.

She swiveled her head and saw all the police officers as they made it out of the garage. The officers instructed them to cross the street, moving a safe distance away from the building as fire trucks began pulling up outside.

"Where are the others?" Cindy asked no one in particular.

"Who?" Viola asked.

Cindy looked around some more. "Carson, Tanner, and Stanley. I don't see them."

"Maybe they got out of the building faster than the rest of us," Ezra suggested.

"I doubt it, not without a police escort at any rate," Cindy said, squinting and looking up and down the street. About fifty feet away what had to be the rest of the hotel's patrons were standing in clusters with a couple of police officers keeping watch over them.

She pushed her way to the edge of her own group so she could get close to one of the police officers who had escorted them from the building. "Three jurors aren't here," she told him.

He scowled and looked at a clipboard in his hand. Then he looked at the group. "Okay, everyone, roll call. Shout out nice and loud so I can hear you."

He rattled down the list of names and sure enough, Carson, Tanner, and Stanley weren't there. The officer grabbed his radio. "We have 3 jurors unaccounted for," he said tersely into it. He followed that up with their names and room numbers.

Cindy couldn't help but wonder where they were and if they were alright. Given the secret she knew about what had happened to Wyatt she could feel her mind starting to go to dark places, wondering if the other three, or at least two of them, were also dead. Her thoughts moved quickly to Jeremiah and she sent up a prayer for his safety.

~

Jeremiah had already searched two rooms and was halfway through his third. His gloves back on, he had moved swiftly and silently to try and cover as much ground as possible before someone else might return to the floor. As much as he hated the blaring of the alarm he was also grateful to it for the concealment it brought.

He finally finished checking the last spot in that room, the ceiling in the bathroom. Like the first two he'd been in the last few minutes this one also appeared to be free of anything of interest.

He made his way back into the hall, easing the door closed. He glanced toward the common area of the floor and then blinked in surprise.

Someone was on the phone.

Before Jeremiah could take a step the figure turned, as if sensing his stare. Then, quick as a flash, bolted for the elevator.

Jeremiah sprinted forward but the elevator doors shut before he could get there. He punched the button to call the elevator as his mind raced through a series of calculations.

If the person had gone down they ran the risk of being seen and identified as they exited the elevator. It would be easy for someone to say who the last person down off the floor was.

On the other hand, it was possible that whoever it was had figured out what Jeremiah had. Although the elevator only traveled down to the garage, bypassing the lobby and all other floors, it did also go up one floor to the restaurant The Top of the World, where guests of this floor had a private entrance to the restaurant. It was how the room service waiters accessed the floor.

The elevator returned mere seconds later and he prayed that his hunch was right as he leaped inside and hit the small, discrete button that would take him to the restaurant.

Moments later he was stepping off the elevator near the back of the restaurant. A small podium stood empty. Jeremiah walked forward quickly but cautiously. Several tables held the remains of dinners that had to be abandoned once the alarm sounded.

It looked like all the diners and staff had evacuated. He made his way toward the bank of elevators that had access to all the floors. A sudden crash and the sound of breaking china on his left pulled his attention that way. He scanned the room, taking several quick steps in that direction but could see no movement.

He turned back just in time to see someone dive into an open elevator. Jeremiah ran forward but was too late to catch it. He pushed the button and seconds later the door to a second elevator opened. While it was possible that whoever he was pursuing would choose to get off on one of the other guest floors, chances were good that whoever it was wanted or needed to get out of the building.

Jeremiah hit the button for the lobby and bolted out the doors the moment the elevator arrived. The lobby was empty except for three firemen. "Hey, you need to get out of here!" one of them shouted to him.

"Did someone else just come down in an elevator?" Jeremiah asked.

"No."

Jeremiah ran around to where the stairs were and yanked the door open. He stepped into the stairwell and looked up. There was no one above him.

A hand descended on his shoulder and he spun around. One of the firefighters stepped back, hands up. “Look, you can’t be here until we check the building.”

Frustration seethed in him. He didn’t know if the person he had been pursuing was the same one from outside the courthouse or not. He had lost them, though, and the opportunity to continue searching the rooms upstairs.

~

Mark and Liam were in the parking garage with another officer when the message came over the radio the other man was carrying that three jurors were unaccounted for.

“There aren’t any officers still in the hotel, are there?” Liam asked.

“No, we were the last three out,” the other man said.

“Which means we’re the ones going back in,” Mark growled.

He didn’t like this, not one bit.

“At least we don’t have to search the entire hotel since we know they could only access the parking garage and their floor via the elevator or stairs,” Liam said.

Mark knew that should be true, but he was still wondering how Jeremiah had accessed the floor. Maybe there was another way. He thought about room service being delivered to the floor. Surely they didn’t have to leave the hotel and go into the parking garage to get to the floor. There must be a way to override the elevator controls to allow it to stop on a floor which would give easy access to the kitchens.

He turned to the uniformed officer. "Get hold of somebody in charge at the hotel and find out how employees like room service waiters access the floor."

"I'm on it," the man said.

"And stay out here and let us know if anyone comes down the elevator," Mark added.

The man nodded and Mark and Liam entered the stairwell and began the long climb up. They had made it about halfway when Liam asked, "Do you think that Jeremiah's out of the building already?"

"I wish I knew," Mark admitted.

"Three people missing. I hope they're just heavy sleepers," Liam said.

"So do I, but what are the odds?"

They finished the rest of the stairs in silence which was good because Mark was getting a little winded toward the end. He was getting out of shape he realized, noticing that his partner seemed just fine. He had no idea what to expect when they opened the door so he had his hand on his gun just in case.

The common area on the floor was empty. The alarms were still going off and it set his nerves on edge. It would also make it nearly impossible to hear someone sneaking up on them.

"Time to start checking rooms," Mark said.

"Two of the rooms are to the left," Liam said.

The wing where Cindy and Wyatt's rooms were. Also the most likely wing to house the killer.

"Which two?"

"Carson and Tanner."

“Okay, let’s go slow and be careful,” Mark muttered.

His instincts were telling him that something was deeply wrong. He drew his gun, not wanting to be caught unprepared in case the trouble he was expecting materialized. Liam did the same as they eased down the hallway.

Liam stopped in front of the first door. He pounded on it hard and called out. They waited ten seconds that seemed to last forever then Liam slipped the master keycard out of his pocket and opened the door.

Mark rushed inside while Liam covered him. It only took a second to realize that there was no one there. The television was on but the room was empty. On the nightstand was a man’s wallet and the jury summons with Carson’s name on it.

Mark picked up the jury summons and stared at it for a moment. The weight and texture of the paper in his hand felt familiar. It was as though he could literally feel his mind working out a problem, but he just couldn’t see the solution yet.

“So, no Carson here,” Liam said, interrupting his train of thought.

Mark dropped the jury summons back on the nightstand. “Let’s check Tanner’s room.”

They eased back into the hallway and across the hall to Tanner’s room. Again Liam made a fist and pounded with no response.

This time Mark yanked open the door and Liam rushed inside. Mark followed close behind him and then came to an abrupt halt.

Tanner was wearing one of the hotel robes and he lay sprawled motionless, face down on the bed.

16

"Is he dead?" Mark asked, throat constricting.

Liam stepped forward cautiously and shook Tanner's shoulder. With a shout the man jerked and sat up, wild-eyed. He stared for a moment at Mark and Liam, his face turning ashen. Then he reached up and pulled earbuds out of his ears. The music coming through the earbuds was so loud that Mark had no problem hearing it halfway across the room despite the alarm going off.

"What are you...is that an alarm? What's happening?" Tanner asked.

Mark relaxed slightly. "Fire alarm. Come with us."

Tanner scrambled to his feet and followed them out into the corridor. The door had just closed when he said, "Wait! I forgot my key."

"Someone will let you back in, just move," Mark growled. They didn't have time to waste on the man since he wasn't dead or involved in killing someone.

Back in the common area they sent him down the stairs after alerting the officer in the parking garage to expect him. They shut the door to the stairwell after him and then crossed over to the other wing.

They stopped in front of Stanley's door. Mark could feel the tension running through his shoulders as Liam lifted his hand and knocked. As with the other two there was no answer.

They burst inside to find the room empty. They searched it quickly then moved back into the hallway.

"We still have two missing jurors. What now?" Liam asked.

"Now, we search all the other rooms," Mark said. "And if we still can't find them we call in forensics and pray there are no more bodies in the ceilings."

Before Liam could respond his radio crackled to life.

~

Cindy's anxiety levels were mounting as she stood huddled together with the others. Where could the three missing jurors be? After seeing Wyatt's skeleton her mind was conjuring up all sorts of gruesome scenarios wherein one, two, or all three of them were dead.

Three isn't very likely. The third would probably be the killer, she thought to herself.

From where she was standing she could see firemen entering and exiting the building. She was betting the alarm was a false one. Possibly just an excuse to get them all outside. For what purpose, though?

Her stomach growled and she was reminded that in all the chaos and stress she had gone to bed without having dinner. She sighed. So much for trying to get some rest. If they let them back into the hotel she'd have to order some room service which meant she wouldn't be getting back to sleep anytime soon.

Joyce yawned so Cindy realized she wasn't the only one who was tired. Prudence and Tara were both shivering. It was cold outside, somewhere in the upper 40s most likely. Prudence's negligee wasn't enough to keep her warm for anything. Tara wore slacks and a blouse that covered every inch of her, but they looked thin.

Jordan noticed Tara shivering, too. "It's okay, we'll be going back in soon, I'm sure," he told her. He put his hand on her shoulder.

Tara leaped away from him like a frightened animal. "Don't touch me!" she shrieked.

"Whoa," Jordan said, taking a step back and looking just as shocked as Cindy felt.

Mike quickly stepped up. "Miss, are you alright?" he asked Tara, standing close but clearly being careful not to touch her.

"F-f-fine," she stammered, clearly upset and embarrassed.

Cindy felt bad for her, but quickly had to check her natural impulse to reach out to her. Something told her Tara didn't want anyone touching her.

"What's wrong?" a male voice asked from behind her.

Cindy turned to see Carson standing there, with a white towel wrapped around his waist and skin and hair wet. Before she could say anything about his sudden appearance he winced. "Sorry, I was in the shower and didn't hear the alarm going off until I turned the water off. I ran out here and didn't even get a chance to put on shoes."

Cindy looked down at his bare feet.

"That had to have hurt," she said, lacking for something better to say.

The truth was she was just relieved to see that he was alright and not another victim of whoever it was that had killed Wyatt.

“Only two missing now,” she murmured.

Carson frowned. “Missing? I was hardly missing, just slow. Who is missing?”

“Tanner and Stanley still.”

“That’s odd.”

“Maybe they got caught in the shower, too, but are taking the time to dress,” Cindy said so as not to worry him. She herself didn’t believe that for a moment.

~

Mark felt marginally better as he and Liam searched room by room. They had heard from the officers downstairs that Tanner had made it down safely. Apparently Carson had also shown up. It sounded like they just missed him somehow. Mark figured they’d sort out all those details later. At least he knew they were both safe. Now if they could just find Stanley and get out of the hotel things would be looking up.

They had just entered the last room and found nothing when the radio crackled to life again.

“Did you find Stanley?” Liam asked.

“Not yet, but fire officials are fairly certain it was a false alarm. They’ll clear the building in about another fifteen minutes. Oh and there’s a rabbi down here waiting to see you.”

“Thanks,” Liam said. Then he turned to look at Mark. “Well, that answers our question. Jeremiah found a way out.”

“The question is did Stanley find the same way out?” Mark asked. “There’s nothing more we can do on this floor. We might as well go down and see what he's found out."

Downstairs Jeremiah was waiting for them, a look of frustration on his face. The three of them moved away from the officer guarding the elevator and stairwell.

"Okay, what happened?" Mark asked.

"I had started checking rooms. I finished with the third one, came out, and saw someone using the phone in the common area."

"Was it a man or a woman?"

"I couldn't tell, they were wearing another one of those hoodies."

"So you think it might have been the same person you chased in front of the courthouse?"

"I can't say for certain, but they certainly gave me the slip like the other one did."

"Mind if I ask how?" Mark asked, struggling to keep the sarcasm out of his voice. Mostly the snarkiness he was feeling was a cover up for the very real fear that was gnawing at his insides. For someone to give Jeremiah the slip meant that the officers on the force would probably have no prayer of catching this guy unless he got sloppy or they caught a break.

"There's an unmarked button in the elevator that takes you to the restaurant upstairs. I chased him up there and then down the regular elevators. I don't know which floor he got off on, but the firemen caught me in the lobby and he hadn't been by them. By the time I was able to check the main stairwell there was no one in it so I couldn't even tell you for sure if he's still in the building or not."

"And since he knew about the button he could have gotten onto the floor that way so we don't even know if he was one of our jurors. Great."

"If he wasn't a juror, why sneak onto the floor just to use the phone?" Liam asked. "If he needed to report in to someone wouldn't he or she have used their own phone?"

"That would make sense," Jeremiah said.

"So, in order for it to make sense that he was using that phone he had to be someone without access to a phone of his own, like our jurors," Mark said. "So, we're back to thinking a juror is behind...everything."

"There are a lot of different strands and it's hard to see where they all interconnect," Liam said.

"Well, whoever it was tonight, they had to have a card that could access the elevator," Jeremiah said.

"Only officers are supposed to have those. Don't tell me it was a police officer that you were chasing after," Mark said. It wouldn't be the first time one of their own had betrayed them, but the thought still made his stomach twist.

"I don't think so. A few key hotel staff have those cards, too," Jeremiah noted. "It wouldn't have been too hard to acquire one."

"One more thing to worry about," Liam said grimly.

"We've got a missing juror," Mark informed Jeremiah.

"Which one?" Jeremiah asked.

"Stanley. Maybe he's the person you were chasing," Mark said. "That would explain his absence."

"What can you tell me about him?" Jeremiah asked.

"Not much. I haven't personally met all the jurors and I'm not entirely sure which of the guys he is."

There was sudden shouting from the entrance to the parking garage.

"What is it?" Mark called.

"We found him! We found Stanley."

Mark broke into a jog and headed for the entrance, wondering in what condition they had found Stanley. Jeremiah and Liam were right behind him.

When he got to the entrance he was both surprised and relieved to see Stanley standing there, a look of guilt on his wrinkled face as an officer held him by the arm.

"Where did you find him?" Mark asked.

"A phone booth a block away."

"I was calling my wife. I was the first person downstairs and I saw my opportunity. It's impossible to have a private conversation with people listening," Stanley said, flushing. "We've been married fifty years and because of this stupid trial we've had our only nights apart in all those years."

Mark wasn't sure whether to laugh or shout. Jeremiah came up beside him. "No chance this is the person you were chasing is there?" Mark asked.

Jeremiah looked at the old man and shook his head.

"Didn't think we could get that lucky. Can't blame a guy for hoping."

"I know I wasn't supposed to, but I'm not sorry I did it," Stanley said defiantly.

Mark sighed. He didn't blame the older gentleman. He was pretty sure in his shoes he would have done something similar.

"At least now everyone's accounted for," Liam said.

"Come on, Stanley, let's go join the others," Mark said.

The officer let go of Stanley's arm and the old man turned obediently to follow Mark. Jeremiah and Liam walked with them. When they arrived at the group Mark looked them over wondering which of them could potentially be a killer. He glanced at Jeremiah and could tell from the way the rabbi was staring intently from face to face that he was trying to figure out the same thing.

The fire chief walked up to the group. "Who's in charge here?" he asked.

Mark winced. That was a good question. "I guess you could say I am for the moment," he answered.

The chief nodded. "Everything's okay. It was a false alarm. I've notified hotel management and they're letting people back inside. The manager asked me to notify you as well since you're handling this group separately from the rest of the hotel guests."

"Thank you, Chief, we appreciate that," Mark said.

The man nodded and left.

Mark turned to the officers present. "Okay, let's get everyone back to the twelfth floor. I want one guard for every two jurors. Let's not lose anyone on the way back in, okay?"

Heads bobbed up and down and then the first officer began leading two of the women back to the parking garage. Two by two they went.

"Just like Noah's ark," Mark muttered to himself.

Cindy was one of the last two to leave and she cast a longing look back over her shoulder at Jeremiah who lifted his hand and waved.

"I can't let you stay. If I do word will get out and everyone will be breathing down my neck demanding that their significant other be allowed to stay, too."

"I understand," Jeremiah said quietly.

"You understand but will you obey?" Mark asked.

Jeremiah gave a short, harsh laugh. “Not very good on the obeying thing. But I can respect a friend’s wishes...for now.”

“Well, as that friend I appreciate that.”

Jeremiah turned and walked down the street. Mark and Liam headed back to the hotel. Once on the twelfth floor they verified that all the jurors were there and in their rooms.

As quiet descended Mark felt a wall of exhaustion hit him. “It’s been a long day,” he said.

“That it has. We should go home and get some rest. I don’t think either of us is capable of much more rational thought at the moment,” Liam said.

“I hate to admit it, but you’re right. My brain’s just starting to go around in circles which definitely isn’t helpful. Hopefully tomorrow we’ll be able to get some perspective on all of this and figure out what’s really going on and why.”

“And not to mention who,” Liam added.

“Exactly,” Mark said, barely suppressing a yawn.

A few minutes later Mark was on his way home, so bleary eyed he could barely stay awake on the road. He kept going over the case in his head, trying to see every angle, partly because he hoped to see something new but mostly to keep his brain occupied enough that he didn’t fall asleep driving.

When he made it home Traci greeted him with a warm smile and a kiss.

“It’ll just take me a bit to heat up your dinner,” she said.

“Thank you,” he told her. He grabbed a small bottle of orange juice out of the refrigerator and started guzzling it, hoping it would wake him up a bit.

"So, more excitement today?" she asked as he sat down wearily at the kitchen table.

"Yeah. Found what we think was the guy who was stabbed in the alley in a field minus hands and head."

"Gross, but okay."

"A juror went missing and then turned up dead."

Traci's eyes went wide. "Who?"

"No one you know," he reassured her.

"Do you know who killed him or why?"

"Not a clue. Except I have a sneaking suspicion it was one of the other jurors. Although, frankly, I'm less sure of that than I was a couple of hours ago."

"Oh? What happened a couple of hours ago?"

"Fire alarm went off at the hotel and everyone had to be evacuated. Three jurors were missing and unaccounted for for several minutes."

"That's not good."

"No, and the one was caught on the phone, supposedly calling his wife."

"Isn't there any way you can tell for sure?"

"Tomorrow I'll request records from the phone company and see if I can work something out," he said.

"What else? There's clearly more. I can tell just by looking at you."

"Perceptive as always. Someone was on the twelfth floor when they shouldn't have been and they were using the phone. I'm also going to pull those records in the morning. Jeremiah gave chase, but, whoever it was, they got away from him."

"That's...disturbing," Traci said in a very controlled voice.

"Tell me about it. It's bad enough that I worry sometimes about having him around my cases. Can you imagine an evil twin of his?"

"A doppelganger. Now that would be terrifying," Traci said with a shudder.

"Anyway, there's something bugging me, like it's just there beneath the surface and I can't quite get a good enough look at what it is."

"You need some sleep."

Mark yawned. "Tell me about it."

Traci pulled a plate out of the microwave and set it before him. "So, as soon as you eat I want you to go to bed."

"Yes ma'am."

He scarfed down his food. He hadn't really eaten anything since the donut that he'd had that morning. Then he meekly followed Traci to the bedroom where they started getting prepared for bed.

Halfway through brushing his teeth he awoke, realizing that he'd taken a micronap of a second or two. He hadn't had things this bad since his college days. He blinked furiously as he tried to get the brain fog to lift long enough that he could finish up his nightly routine.

When he made it back into the bedroom he discovered that Traci had not only beaten him to bed but had also fallen asleep already. He laid down gingerly, trying not to wake her. He realized he hadn't had a chance to go in and kiss the twins goodnight.

They were probably already asleep, though, and he didn't want to risk waking them. Particularly not with Traci already asleep. She needed the rest even more than he did.

He turned out the light, got cozy under the covers, and let his mind drift. Images from the day, snatches of conversations began to bombard him. He didn't want to think of those things and he tried to push them from his mind. Finally he managed to do so and he sunk down into peaceful slumber.

Mark sat straight up in bed and turned on the light as something suddenly hit him. Traci stirred and opened one eye to look up at him. "What is it?" she asked.

"I have an idea...it's terrible, but I think I'm right."

"What idea?" she said, sitting up herself.

"Today when I was in one of the juror's rooms I picked up his jury summons and something struck me about the feel of the paper. It was familiar, but I couldn't put my finger on it. It felt and looked the same as a scrap of torn paper found at that crime scene, the one where the body was moved."

"What are you saying?"

"I think the dead guy had a jury summons on him and that whoever killed him took it and then took his place. I think one of the jurors is an imposter."

17

"Are you sure?" Traci asked, alarm clear in her voice.

"Sure enough that I'm going to go in to the station and check out that scrap of paper again. If I'm right this could also help identify the dead guy. He's someone who was called up for jury duty this week and I'd be willing to bet he's one of the seven men that got selected. There's only six of them now."

"And didn't you say that three of them were missing for a while during the fire alarm?"

"Yes, we'll focus on those three first. Then the other three."

"But what if the imposter was the guy who was murdered in his hotel room?" Traci asked.

"Then this thing just gets weirder and weirder."

"Shouldn't you call Cindy and warn her that she might be trapped in that hotel with a killer?"

"She already knows that's a possibility. Besides, I can't call the shared phone and get a police officer to wake her up in the middle of the night without the risk of raising someone's suspicions. No, I'm going to call Jeremiah. He can get to her while I get to the police station."

Mark lunged out of bed and reached for his clothes. The more he thought about it the more it made sense. The killer had needed there to be a delay in discovering the murdered man's identity so that he could continue to masquerade as him during the trial. To what purpose, though? To try and sway the jury? To get close to Jason Todd? There'd already been a couple of attempts on the man's life. Maybe someone was desperate enough to kill him that they didn't care who else got hurt in the process.

He tripped trying to get his pants on and smacked his shin on the bedpost. He bit back an oath.

"What can I do?" Traci asked.

"Actually you can call Jeremiah and tell him to go to the hotel. Call Liam and tell him to meet me at the station," he said as he finally pulled his pants on.

"On it," she said as she snatched up the phone.

Mark had reached the front door and could hear Traci explaining things to Jeremiah as he headed out. In the car he kept blinking, his vision still fuzzy from sleep even as he sped down the deserted streets.

More questions filled his mind and he realized that even if he was right about this it was just the tip of the iceberg. Who had caused the car to crash with four jurors in it? It couldn't have been the imposter. And no one could have known which jurors were riding in which cars so it wasn't like somebody was trying to kill him. Was it possible the two things were unrelated? Were there possibly two people trying to sabotage the trial? Or more?

His head was throbbing by the time he made it to the station. He swung by his desk to grab some Tylenol he kept in the drawer, forcing himself to dry swallow them because he didn't want to waste time getting water.

He turned around and shouted in surprise. Liam was standing there, holding an evidence bag containing the scrap of paper in question.

"What the devil? How did you get here before me?" Mark demanded.

"I was already here when Traci called, going over some of my notes. It kept bothering me, the fact that the car accident and the murder of Wyatt didn't seem to fit together. I had just come to the conclusion that there might be two different perpetrators. Although to what end I have no idea."

"Great minds think alike."

"They've already dusted this for prints and only got a partial that they couldn't use," Liam said as he pulled the scrap of paper out of the plastic bag.

Mark picked it up and looked at it. "I'd be willing to bet money that this came from a jury summons. The paper's thick, somewhat distinctive."

"There are lots of thick papers, lots of things printed on cardstock," Liam said.

"Yeah, but my gut is telling me that's what this is."

"Fortunately we don't have to rely on your gut."

Mark turned around to see Vaughn standing there, holding a cup of coffee and yawning.

"What are you doing here?" he asked the forensics expert.

"Liam called me."

"So what do we need to do?"

"We can match the paper to the paper they use for jury summons. We should be able to get close enough to determine if that's what you have."

"Now we just need a jury summons," Mark said, thinking they were going to need to make a trip to the hotel.

Vaughn pulled one out of his pocket. "You're in luck. My wife's misfortune is your fortune. This just came in today's mail. She's got jury duty coming up on her birthday."

"Then what are we waiting for?" Mark asked. "Let's get this thing tested."

~

Jeremiah didn't have the time or the patience for subtlety. That's why he had opted to take the direct approach when it came to dealing with getting into the hotel. He avoided the guards in the parking garage and instead made his way through the lobby, into the elevator, and up to the restaurant. He then crossed to the private elevator and rode it down one floor.

When the doors opened he had pressed himself against one of the front facing panels in such a way that the police officer on guard duty wouldn't see him, but would instead just see an empty elevator. He waited a couple seconds to make sure the officer had time to observe the seemingly empty elevator car then he pressed the up button.

When he came down a second time he held the door open button and waited for the officer to stand up and come closer to inspect the elevator to see what was wrong with it. He could judge by the man's footsteps when he was right where he wanted him. Three more steps and he'd be able to see Jeremiah.

Jeremiah hit send on his phone and the telephone on the table behind the officer rang. The man stopped as Jeremiah had expected him to, then he heard the rustle of clothing as the man turned to face the phone.

On silent feet Jeremiah stepped quickly forward out of the elevator and hit the nerve cluster where the man's neck met his shoulder. It rendered the officer instantly unconscious and also locked up his muscles to keep him standing upright. It would be several minutes before he regained consciousness and when he did he wouldn't quite know what had happened to him.

Jeremiah made his way to Cindy's room and knocked lightly on the door, not wanting to wake up her neighbors. She didn't answer so he used the master keycard he'd obtained for himself earlier from an unsuspecting maid and entered the room.

As soon as he had closed the door he said, "Cindy, it's Jeremiah, wake up."

He heard a slight groan and then "Jeremiah?"

He turned on the light and walked all the way into the room. Cindy was staring up at him from the bed, her hair fanned out around her head like a halo. "What's going on?"

"Mark thinks he might have made a breakthrough in the case. He wanted me to come here and be with you," Jeremiah said as he sat down on the edge of the bed and looked down at her.

She was so beautiful and she looked so innocent when she was sleepy. He had to remind himself that was because she really was one of the most innocent people he knew. All the serial killers, murderers, terrorists, and bad guys hadn't been able to take that away from her and he loved it.

"I was having a really good dream," she said.

"Really, what was it about?" he asked.

"I was dreaming about our wedding."

"That does sound like a good dream."

"You looked so handsome. And there was snow."

"Snow? It doesn't snow in Pine Springs. Not since I've been here."

"It did once when I was a little girl. It was in December and we were vacationing at The Zone."

He felt his heart skip a beat. "December. Is that when you want to get married?"

"I was thinking about it, but December of next year. We don't need to rush, and we have a lot of things to plan for. We'll probably have to plan that far out because December is such a busy month."

He took a deep breath. It seemed forever away, but he could be patient if that's what she wanted. He picked up her left hand and kissed her ring. "Alright, December of next year it is," he said with a smile.

Cindy struggled up to a sitting position and gave him a quick kiss before getting out from under the covers and heading for the bathroom. She'd been in there for only a couple of seconds when she popped back out, a frown on her face.

"What's wrong?" he asked.

"These towels. The towels here in the bathroom. They're green."

"Yes? So what?" Jeremiah asked.

"Normally hotel guest rooms have white towels. I think because they're easier to keep looking clean and new, no fading, and they can bleach them easily."

"These look nicer," Jeremiah noted.

"It's not just my room, either. Wyatt's room had green towels."

"I still don't see what you're getting at," Jeremiah said.

"A white towel. It was a white towel that Carson had wrapped around him when he said he'd been in the shower when the alarm went off. Don't you see? He couldn't have been. He had to have gotten that towel from somewhere else."

"The pool area?" Jeremiah suggested.

"Yes! Probably. And it would have been easy for him to get himself wet either in the pool or at one of the places to rinse off."

"So, he was up to something and needed to buy himself some time. I wonder if he was the man I chased?" Jeremiah mused.

"Wait, what man that you chased?" she asked, her voice puzzled.

"After everyone was supposed to have evacuated the building I caught someone on the telephone in the communal area. Whoever it was they got away."

"That seems a bit...odd."

"Mark, Liam, and I thought so, too. They're looking into it."

"Do you think it was Wyatt's killer?"

"I don't know. It's possible," he said.

"Carson, Tanner, and Stanley were the three men that weren't with the rest of us when we first left the hotel. They all eventually showed up. Tanner was apparently asleep and Stanley said he'd snuck off to a pay phone to call his wife."

"So it could have been any of the three of them or someone else entirely," Jeremiah mused.

“What did Mark want us to do?” she asked.

“Just sit tight until further notice, I believe.”

She sighed. “Great, more waiting.”

“We can talk about where you’d like to have the ceremony,” he suggested.

A grin spread across her face.

~

“You know, I moved to Pine Springs because it was supposed to be quiet here,” Vaughn said with a sigh as he looked up from the microscope he had been peering through. “A nice, safe place with not as much to do in the city, not as much stress and pressure.”

“Not finding things as advertised?” Liam asked.

“No, certainly not.”

“What ever is?” Mark asked fighting his grogginess and his growing impatience.

“Still after working in New York City I was expecting more of a break than this,” Vaughn said, moving a slide around on the microscope before looking again.

“We’re within spitting distance of Los Angeles. Sometimes the crazies come to us,” Liam offered.

“And sometimes a middle of the night breakthrough is worth it,” Vaughn mused as he continued to stare through the microscope. He looked up. “You are correct, gentlemen. After running some chemical tests and analyzing the fibers I can say with a fair degree of certainty that the scrap of paper you found was indeed part of a jury summons.”

“Let’s go, we have a killer to grab,” Mark told Liam.

"Wait, this doesn't prove anything," Vaughn protested. "Just that you found a scrap of paper in the same alley where some man was killed."

"Oh, I'd say it proves everything," Liam said.

"But, they send out hundreds of these things each week. More, I imagine, if you count the surrounding areas. We have no idea how old this was or who might have dropped it there. It proves nothing," Vaughn insisted.

"You know what the advantage of living in Pine Springs is?" Mark asked as he and Liam headed out the door.

"What?" Vaughn called after them.

"We're too small a town to have a coincidence that big."

Once in the car Mark had Liam call Jeremiah and fill him in.

"He wants to know what we want Cindy and him to do," Liam said after a minute.

"Nothing. Just keep an eye on her until we get this straightened out. Hopefully we won't need his help and if we do I think it will become exceedingly obvious," Mark said.

Liam relayed the information and finally hung up. A couple minutes later they reached the hotel and were soon exiting the elevator on the twelfth floor.

The officer on duty stood up and Mark noticed the man's head was cocked to the side and he was rubbing his neck. "Detectives, I didn't expect to see you tonight. Is anything wrong?"

"Hopefully not. We just need to ask some of the jurors a couple of questions," Mark said, not ready to discuss their discovery just yet. Odds were it would do no harm, but so close to finding their killer an abundance of caution seemed in order.

"It's awfully late," the officer said with a frown.

"We know. We want to get this over with so we can go home and get some sleep," Liam said with a friendly smile.

"Okay. Let me know if you need anything."

"Of course. Something happen to your neck?" Mark asked.

The officer frowned. "It's a little sore. I...tripped...I guess is what happened and I must have hurt it when I fell. I don't really remember."

"What did you trip on?" Marked asked, suddenly suspicious.

"I'm not really sure, to tell the truth. I went to check on the elevator. I turned around, and...next thing I knew I was on the floor."

"Call in for a replacement if you need to go home," Mark said.

"No, I'm good, sir."

"Okay."

Mark and Liam took a couple of steps away. Mark couldn't shake the feeling that the man hadn't just tripped. He was hoping, though, that whatever had happened to him Jeremiah had been the one behind it.

"Let's start on this side. That means checking Carson, Tanner, and Mike first," Liam said, glancing at the list of rooms.

"I think I'm having déjà vu," Mark said as they stopped outside Carson's door.

"Like we were just here a few hours ago?" Liam asked with a sigh.

Mark glanced at his partner. Liam didn't usually show any signs of mental or physical fatigue, so the tiny sigh from him had the same impact that a full on outburst from someone else would have.

"Are you okay?" he asked.

"Just...lot on my mind," Liam muttered.

"Have anything to do with a certain Miss Tea Thyme?" Mark asked.

"Rebecca?"

"Yes, Rebecca."

"I don't know, maybe."

So, yes, Mark thought but didn't say out loud. The tea shop owner had clearly gotten under Liam's skin. They wouldn't be the first couple in the history of Pine Springs to find romance over a dead body.

"Hold that thought," Mark said. He knocked loudly on the door and waited. He let several seconds pass before knocking again harder.

Carson opened the door and gazed suspiciously out at them. "It's the middle of the night, I was asleep," he said.

Which Mark might have believed if the man hadn't been fully dressed still, shoes and all.

"Sorry to disturb you, but we need to see your jury summons," Mark said.

"My what?"

"The piece of paper you had to bring with you to jury duty at the beginning of the week," Liam said smoothly.

"Oh, that. I don't know if I have it. Hold on."

Carson closed the door. Mark glanced at Liam. "Not very hospitable," he murmured.

Liam shook his head.

A minute passed.

"Do you think we were lucky enough to hit the jackpot first try?" Liam said softly.

"I'm beginning to wonder."

"Think he's going to bolt?"

"Well, we know the windows are sealed shut," Mark whispered, "and I haven't heard any breaking glass."

"He could have tools with him."

"It's possible."

"Or he might be making up his mind whether to go through us," Liam said.

"Exactly what I was thinking," Mark said as he eased his gun out of his holster and took a step back.

Liam took two steps to the side and also pulled his gun.

Mark tensed as he heard a sound at the door. It opened suddenly and Carson thrust the piece of paper out at them with a grunt. He didn't even seem to notice the fact that both officers had their guns drawn.

Mark discretely reholstered his gun and then took the jury summons. It had Carson's name on it and the correct date. More important, it was completely intact.

"Thank you," Mark said, handing it back.

"Hey, what is this all about?" Carson asked.

"Possible clerical error down at the courthouse. We just want to make sure that all you hard working, sacrificing jurors get paid on time for your service," Liam said without missing a beat.

Carson guffawed. "The couple of bucks a day we get paid? The city can keep it. It's not even worth the bother of trying to cash the dang thing."

"You're always free to waive the payment," Liam said. "Make sure you talk to the clerk about that."

Carson rolled his eyes. "If there's nothing else?"

"Have a good rest of your night, sir," Mark said.

Carson closed the door and Mark and Liam crossed the hall.

"I had no idea you could spread the bull that thick," Mark commented.

"I'm Irish and we call it blarney."

"I call it astounding that he believed it."

Mark raised his fist and knocked on Tanner's door. "We better not find him faceplanted on his bed again," he muttered.

Seconds later the door opened and Tanner stared at them with a baffled look on his face. "Is it morning already?" he slurred.

"Not quite. We just need to clear up a couple of administrative details that got overlooked in all the excitement. May we see your jury summons?" Mark asked.

"My jury summons? Why?"

"The clerk was supposed to check them all in on Wednesday but with the car accident and everything...well, you know bureaucracy," Liam said.

"Oh, sure, yeah, that makes sense. One second."

He turned and shuffled into the room. Mark caught the door to keep it from closing. He angled himself so he could see most of the room. Tanner went first to the table, then to the dresser, then disappeared next to the bed, presumably checking the nightstand. He finally came back frowning.

"I can't find it. I must have left it at the house on Tuesday when I went home to pack. It's important, you say?"

"Yes, but we can have someone run you over to your house tomorrow to get it," Liam said.

"Okay, thank you," Tanner said with a yawn.

"Have a good rest of your night," Liam said.

They turned to go and Tanner closed the door behind him.

"No use in dragging him to his house until we've checked the other four," Liam said.

"I agree."

They came to Mike's door and knocked on it. After several seconds the man opened the door, squinting against the light in the hallway. Behind him his room was pitch black.

"What's wrong? Is the fire real after all?" he asked with a yawn.

"No fire. Sorry to disturb you. There was a clerical foul up and we need to check everyone's jury summons," Mark said, trying to sound apologetic.

"And that couldn't wait until morning?" Mike asked, his voice quickly taking on a suspicious edge.

"We wouldn't have woken you if it wasn't important. We need to get this dealt with before morning," Liam said.

Mike squinted at him. "Sounds like a bunch of bull," he said.

"Do you have it with you?" Mark asked, struggling to keep an edge out of his voice.

"Sure I've got it. Wait here."

Mike closed the door and a few seconds later opened it again.

"Here."

Mike produced his jury summons and Mark felt a thrill of discovery. The summons had been torn into many small pieces and then taped back together.

18

Mark reached out for Mike's jury summons and out of the corner of his eye he could see Liam slowly reaching for his gun, clearly trying to not draw attention to himself as he did so.

"My youngest is going through a tear everything up phase," Mike said, suddenly sounding apologetic. "We try to keep things out of her reach but this must have fallen off the table because I found her happily shredding it. I put it back together as best I could. I was just glad I could still read my juror number."

Mark's heart sank when he realized that messy as the whole thing was, all four corners were present and intact. He showed it to Liam who then eased his hand away from his gun.

"Sounds like she's a handful," Mark said as he handed back the summons. He couldn't help but wonder if that was the kind of thing he and Traci had to look forward to.

"She is, but she can also be a little angel sometimes." Mike took back the summons. "Is there anything else you need?" he asked.

"No, sorry to disturb you so late."

They turned and headed back down the hallway. Mark could hear Mike close his door. For a moment he thought of stopping at Cindy's room but realized that he really did need her and Jeremiah to stay put while they handled this.

"Three down, three to go," he said.

Liam nodded.

When they passed through the common area Mark noticed that the officer was still rubbing his neck. He really was going to have to ask Jeremiah if he knew anything about that.

The first door they came to belonged to a man named Ezra. Mark hadn't heard anything about him really. He knocked on the door and after a few seconds the door opened to reveal an older gentleman with a kindly face who looked at them in surprise.

"How can I help you gentlemen?" he asked.

Mark gave him the same spiel they'd given the first three men.

Ezra tilted his head and looked at him thoughtfully for a moment then finally spoke. "You know, I don't believe a word of that. But I do believe you have a good reason for asking. Come in."

Mark glanced at Liam and then the two followed Ezra into his room. The covers on his bed were askew and the light on the nightstand burned feebly. Ezra turned on another light and then moved over to the table at the far end of the room. He picked something up from it and then walked back over to Mark and Liam.

He held out a paper airplane. "I'm sorry. I got a little bored after dinner," he said sheepishly.

Mark took the airplane and carefully unfolded it. When he had, he found that the summons was perfectly intact.

"Thank you," he said as he handed it back to Ezra.

"Don't suppose you're going to tell me what this is really about?" the other man asked.

"Just paperwork," Mark said, forcing a smile.

"Well, I hope you find what it is you're looking for."

"Thank you," Liam said.

They quickly exited Ezra's room and moved on to Jordan's.

Mark knocked again. He had to admit to himself that it was getting tedious but his nerves were also strung a bit tight. After all, if he was right, then one of these last two men had to have a torn summons. If they didn't...well, he'd have to cross that bridge when he came to it.

The door opened and a tall, thin man wearing a Superman T-shirt stood there, wide-eyed. "Can I help you?" he asked.

"Yes, due to a mixup at the courthouse we need to look at your jury summons," Mark said, getting too frustrated and anxious to put it more smoothly.

"Oh, okay, sure."

He turned and walked back into the room. Mark caught the door and took a couple of steps after him. Liam joined him.

Mark watched in mounting anticipation as Jordan searched for his jury summons.

"I know it's here somewhere," he said as he rechecked his suitcase for the third time.

There was a stack of comic books on the table and the second time he went over to the table he actually started sorting through the books instead of just moving the stack.

"Here it is!" he said, sounding overly relieved.

Even before he handed it to Mark the detective saw what he'd been looking for. The top right corner of the summons was torn off.

"Do you have your driver's license on you?" Liam asked as Mark slipped a bag out of his jacket pocket to deposit the summons in.

"No, I think I left it at home when I was packing. I was looking for it earlier today but I didn't find it. What's all this about?"

"You don't seem too concerned that you're missing your license," Mark commented.

"The room, food, everything is paid for and we're not allowed to go anywhere or do anything so it's not like I need it until I get home. Can you tell me what's going on?"

"We're going to need you to come with us and answer a few questions," Mark said.

Jordan blinked at him. "No way, what is this? Who are you guys?"

"Detectives," Mark said, showing him his badge. "And we need you to come with us."

Mark stared into Jordan's eyes, watching to see if the man was going to try and run or fight. Instead he just stared back, eyes wide in alarm.

"Am I under arrest?"

"No, but you will be if you don't cooperate."

~

Cindy waited with bated breath as Jeremiah answered his phone. At this time of the night it could only be Mark calling to update them. When he finally hung up he seemed to relax slightly.

"Well?" she asked.

"They think they got the right guy. Someone named Jordan."

Cindy frowned.

"What's wrong?" he asked.

"That doesn't seem right. I don't buy him as a killer," she said.

"No?"

"No."

"Why not?"

"I don't know. He just seems like a nice guy. And I know, appearances can be deceiving, but it just doesn't feel right to me. Besides, I think he's at the other end of the floor and I don't see how he could have just casually walked past the police officer in the common area carrying a duffel bag with toxic chemicals in it. Wouldn't the officer on duty remember having seen him? Not to mention he'd be walking back without the duffel."

"The second time could have been after the officers changed shifts," Jeremiah suggested.

"Yeah, but then two different officers would have to conveniently not remember seeing him the night before Wyatt turned up missing."

"It would be possible to pull off, but not easy, especially without raising some sort of suspicion," Jeremiah admitted.

"No, I'm convinced that whoever killed Wyatt is on this side of the floor," Cindy said.

"Okay, and who's on that list?"

"Aside from me, there's Prudence. She's the mayor's wife, though, and I don't see her lifting a finger to do something like that herself."

"Wouldn't want to get her hands dirty?" Jeremiah asked.

"It's not that. She's too lazy," Cindy said.

"Okay, who else is on this side?"

"Tanner, who's been acting strangely this entire time. He wanted to get on the jury. He even lied and said he didn't know anything about the case when he clearly did. And he's been trying to get other jurors to talk about the case during our breaks which is against the rules."

"Plus he was talking to Isaac when he had the heart attack," Jeremiah said. "It appeared that the conversation was somewhat heated."

"But he was with me in the car that morning so he couldn't have caused the car crash."

"No, but he could have orchestrated it. Or someone could have been trying to get to him."

"No one should have been able to figure out who was in which car. If he did manage to tip someone off, why would he orchestrate the car crash? There was a very real chance he could have been seriously hurt in it."

"To cause chaos? To allow him the opportunity to talk to that reporter and possibly even kill him?"

"It just seems like a risky move. Too many variables to be sure he'd get the outcome he wanted if that was the case," Cindy said. "Paramedics or police could have immediately isolated him keeping him from interacting with the reporter."

"True. Okay, who do we have next?"

"There's Mike. He seems a decent guy. He stuck up for Joyce when Wyatt was being a jerk. He also saved me from falling down the stairs when I stubbed my toe during the fire alarm."

"Was there an altercation between him and Wyatt?" Jeremiah asked.

"No, nothing like that."

"Okay, moving on."

"There's Carson. He smuggled a cell phone and one of those smart watches into the courtroom the first day. He was constantly doing something on the watch. They took the phone from him on the second day. He was an alternate until Wyatt went missing. He also was late coming down from the fire alarm wearing a towel he definitely did not get from his room and claiming he'd been in the shower."

"Has he done anything else odd?" Jeremiah asked.

Cindy frowned, concentrating. "Nothing is springing to mind."

"You seem uncertain."

"I feel uncertain. Like there was something I should remember that was important."

"Did he spend much time talking to the other jurors?" Jeremiah asked.

"No, he spent most of Wednesday doing something with his smart watch and most of today writing on what looked like a piece of hotel stationary."

"Do you know what he was writing?"

Cindy shook her head.

"Okay, who does that leave?"

"Joyce, she's a retired Kindergarten teacher, and I don't honestly think she could hurt a fly."

"There's another room in this wing," Jeremiah said.

"That's for the police officers. They have a room each side."

Jeremiah cleared his throat. "I suggest we focus on the three men and the police officers for now."

"You think an officer could be involved?" Cindy asked.

"It wouldn't be the first time. And they'd have a little more unfettered access."

Cindy sighed. "I hate having to be suspicious of them, of anyone, actually."

"I know, but we do know one thing for sure."

"What's that?" she asked.

"Wyatt is dead and someone killed him."

~

Mark was having a hard time keeping his eyes open. He and Liam had spent a couple of hours questioning Jordan and he was pretty convinced that Jordan wasn't their man, despite the fact that he had a torn jury summons. Maybe he had been jumping to conclusions about that in the first place. All that was left to do was retrieve his driver's license from his house to confirm his identity and then they'd probably have to cut him loose.

Which was problematic given that Jordan now knew that Wyatt had been murdered. They were probably going to have to give up on their idea of keeping the trial going until they found the killer. There was a slim chance they could convince Jordan to cooperate, especially since he hadn't called a lawyer yet.

Liam walked over, carrying two cups of coffee and set them down on the desk Mark was sitting at.

"What a mess," he commented.

"Tell me about it," Mark groaned.

"You look terrible."

"So do you."

"What do you think we should do?" Liam asked.

Mark didn't want to make the decision, especially given how tired he was. Before he could say anything, though, Liam straightened.

"Here comes the captain," Liam said. "And he doesn't look happy."

Mark looked up just as the captain stopped in front of them. He was clutching a newspaper in his fist.

"Detectives, we have a big problem."

"What's wrong?" Mark asked.

The captain slammed the newspaper down on Mark's desk and Mark stared at the headline in shock.

TODD TRIAL JUROR MISSING!

19

Mark stared for a moment in disbelief then began to read the story.

One of the jurors for the Jason Todd trial disappeared from his hotel room despite heavy police protection. It is not known at this time what happened to Wyatt Collins or whether foul play was involved. The mood among the remaining jurors is tense with some sharply divided even at this stage of the trial.

The article went on, but Mark had seen enough. He looked at the byline. "Who is Felix Hoskins?" he asked.

"I don't know, but whoever he is, he seems to be on the inside," Liam said.

"Maybe we've just determined the real name of our imposter," the captain growled. "You need to find him and shut this down now."

The captain headed for his office and once there slammed the door shut behind him.

"One of the jurors is selling information to the press," Liam said.

"Or is a member of the press," Mark added.

"Given the publicity around this case wouldn't the attorneys involved screen out members of the press so they couldn't become jurors?"

"Only if they knew someone was a member of the press. This Felix could have lied to make his way onto the jury."

"If that's true he would have had to steal a jury summons, too. Do you think it could be Jordan?"

"Maybe we should go ask him," Mark said grimly.

Liam frowned. "That seems a little crazy to me. To kill someone for their jury summons just so you can hopefully get the inside scoop on a trial and write about it seems weird. It's hard to believe that's enough motivation for murder."

"You and I both know people have killed for far less."

"True, but by actually publishing an article he has to realize that he's going to get caught and end up in jail."

"Maybe the fame or the money or something is worth it to him," Mark said. "Either way, it's time to make a couple of phone calls and find out who the mystery informant is."

~

Cindy woke up with a start and glanced at the clock on the nightstand. It was early. She looked across the room and saw Jeremiah still sitting at the table where she had last seen him before she fell asleep. He was staring off into space, seemingly lost in thought.

"Good morning," she said.

"Good morning," he answered, turning to give her a smile.

"What were you thinking about?" she asked. "Figured out who did it yet?"

"No, I was working on a different problem," he said.

"Anything I can help with?"

He frowned. "I don't know. Marie and I were still trying to work out some details for the Purim celebration before she lost her brother. Now it's up to me to solve a couple of difficulties."

"Tell me what they are. I'm a church secretary so I should be able to help."

"While you and Marie are counterparts, some of our problems I'm not sure you'll have encountered before since you haven't worked for a synagogue."

"Lay them on me anyway. Two heads are better than one."

"Are you familiar with the story of Esther?" Jeremiah asked.

"Sure. The king was angry with his wife and his advisers convinced him to replace her. Esther was one of the young women groomed for the position and she pleased the king and he made her queen. One of the king's advisers, though, hated the Jews, most notably Esther's cousin, Mordecai, who had raised her like his own daughter."

"The name of the king's adviser was Haman," Jeremiah said.

Cindy nodded. "Mordecai had warned Esther not to tell anyone that she was Jewish. Haman convinced the king to set a date wherein the people in his kingdom would slaughter the Jews."

"Yes. Then Mordecai told Esther to beg the king to spare her people. She was afraid but she told Mordecai to gather together all the Jews in the area to fast and pray and she and her maidens would do likewise before she approached the king unbidden," Jeremiah said.

"Wasn't approaching him when you hadn't been summoned risking death?" Cindy asked, trying to remember the details of the story.

"Yes, which was why she was so afraid. She went and he was pleased with her when she came into his presence. She asked him to attend a feast she was putting on for him and to bring Haman with him. At that feast he told her to ask for whatever she wanted, up to half his kingdom. She asked them to attend a feast the next day and then revealed her heritage and that Haman was seeking to kill her people. Haman was hung on the gallows he'd had built for Mordecai, and the Jews were allowed to destroy their oppressors. Many converted to Judaism because of the wonders they saw when God preserved His people."

"So, that's what you're celebrating at Purim," Cindy said.

"The day after the Jews were allowed to fight back and destroy those who would destroy them there was much feasting. The word 'Purim' means 'lots' and is a reference to the fact that Haman drew lots to decide on which day to have the Jews exterminated. Purim is one of the most festive holidays with beauty pageants, carnivals, costume contests. I've heard it referred to as Jewish Mardi Gras."

"That sounds fun," Cindy said, wondering where the difficulties arose for those running the event.

"It is. The Megillah is read, the scroll of Esther, and everyone boos and hisses and makes noise anytime Haman's name is mentioned so as to blot it out."

"So, what is the synagogue doing?"

“We will be having a carnival.”

“And what are the problems that you’re trying to work through?”

“We are commanded to eat, drink, all that. It does get a little dicey, though, because we are instructed to drink until we can no longer tell the difference between the phrases ‘cursed be Haman’ and ‘blessed be Mordecai’.”

“Wow, to not be able to tell the difference between those two you’d have to be really drunk,” Cindy said, unable to hide the surprise in her voice.

“Exactly. Now, not everyone drinks that much, but…”

“But at the same time if someone wants to drink that much you really can’t stop them,” Cindy said.

“Exactly.”

“And suddenly you have people who are at the synagogue, having a good time, and are way too drunk to drive home.”

“Yes,” he said. “We’ve tried several different things. We’ve rented shuttles to take people home this year, but we have no clue how we’re going to get them willingly on the shuttles before they pass out.”

“No one wants to leave a good party?” Cindy asked.

“And I’m fine with that. I just don’t need them passing out on the lawn,” Jeremiah said with a sigh.

“Has that actually happened?”

“Every year I’ve been here,” Jeremiah said.

“How have I never noticed?”

“Because we’ve worked really hard to get everyone home before dawn. I’d like to make things go more smoothly this year. And given that Marie is going to be sitting Shiva next week I won’t have the help I need if things do go crazy.”

"So, how to get people to leave willingly," Cindy mused.

"Yes. If I could figure that out, it would be huge," he said.

"I'll give it some thought and see if I can come up with anything," she said.

"Thank you. I appreciate it."

She nodded and got up. "I wish I knew what was going to happen today. I mean, I doubt we're going to have jury duty. Not if Mark and Liam have arrested Jordan. That's not something you can just gloss over. I should probably get ready, though, just in case."

"If you don't you risk looking like you know more than the others," Jeremiah said. "It may be moot, but better safe than sorry."

"What about you?"

"If you have jury duty I'll leave after the officers escort all of you out. If not, it won't matter so much when I leave."

She nodded. It made sense to her. She just wished she knew what was going on with Mark.

~

Liam had seemingly been on a personal call for the last five minutes, but the tone had quickly changed from friendly to serious. Mark couldn't help but wonder what was going on. Finally Liam hung up with a frown.

"Something wrong?" Mark asked.

"I don't know, maybe," Liam muttered.

"What is it?"

“I have a cousin who works in Vegas, for one of the casinos.”

“Irish mob ties?” Mark joked.

Liam looked at him sharply and Mark regretted the comment. Thoughts of Liam’s mysterious grandfather with the passion for gun collecting instantly came to mind.

“What did your cousin have to say?” Mark asked quickly.

“He noticed something that he thought was unusual…and since it affected my jurisdiction he wanted to give me a heads up.”

“What on earth is it?” Mark asked, his curiosity really aroused.

“Apparently all the major odds makers in Vegas are favoring a conviction for Jason Todd. All except one.”

“Do they always all lock step on things like that?” Mark asked.

“No, but they all were on this one until the one made a sudden change last night and flipped from their original position. Now they’re laying odds that Jason Todd is going to be acquitted.”

“So, what is it that particular odds maker knows that everyone else doesn’t?”

“That’s exactly what my cousin was wondering. He thought it suspicious enough that he wanted to give me a heads up given that the trial is happening here and he knew I was likely involved in security for it.”

“That’s awfully friendly of him.”

Liam gave him a small smile. “It was also very self-interested. If someone has the inside track on what’s happening he wants them caught and shut down before it hurts his business.”

"Good to know."

"Anything back from the paper?"

"Not yet. I think it's time to go down there and shake things up," Mark said.

"Lead the way."

~

Cindy was getting edgy and impatient waiting to find out what the day was going to bring. Finally she kissed Jeremiah goodbye and headed for the common area. When she got there Ezra greeted her.

"Couldn't sleep either?" he asked as she sat down beside him.

She shrugged. "It was a bit of a restless night," she admitted.

"It didn't help that I was awake half the night wondering what those police detectives really wanted," he said.

Inwardly she winced, but fortunately he didn't ask her if she'd had any encounters with them or knew any more than he did.

"So, tell me about your young man," Ezra said with a smile. "He is a rabbi, I understand."

"Yes. He's wonderful," Cindy said, unable to keep from grinning.

"Is he from here?"

"Actually he grew up in Israel."

"Ah, so that should make for some interesting cultural differences," Ezra said.

Spoken by anyone else the words might have had an antagonistic edge to them, but she could tell that Ezra meant no offense by them.

"Every once in a while something will come as a bit of a surprise," Cindy said.

"Are your families supportive?" he asked.

"Mine…I guess so. His, not so much."

"I'm sorry. That can make things difficult."

"Thank you." She took a deep breath and changed the subject. "I've never met a Messianic Jew before."

He chuckled. "I get that a lot. I'd be happy to answer any questions you might have."

Before she could say anything she heard a blood-curdling scream. Cindy leaped to her feet. The scream had come from the direction of her wing of rooms. It had been female which meant either Joyce or Prudence was in trouble.

She started running that direction and the police officer on duty sprinted past her, gun drawn.

She forced herself to slow down, not wanting to get in the officer's way, especially if there was real trouble. She felt a hand grab her arm and she spun around to see Ezra, his look tense.

"Better let him handle this," he said.

What he said made sense, but she couldn't let it go. She kept moving and after a moment Ezra came with her. She heard a door open with a crash and then noticed people in the hallway. She quickly realized that the police officer had disappeared into Prudence's room.

With her heart in her throat Cindy slowed to nearly a crawl and crept closer, listening for sounds of a struggle. What she heard instead was hysterical sobbing.

Cautiously she looked into the room. Prudence was standing, a towel wrapped around her and clutched tight in her hands. She was crying openly and the police officer was on the far side of the room, checking her window.

Between the two of them the floor was strewn with all of Prudence's clothes. The place looked like a bomb had gone off in it.

"What happened?" Cindy asked.

Prudence spun toward her with a gasp of fear and then relaxed slightly when she saw Cindy. "I've been robbed!"

20

Something didn't feel right to Cindy as she stared at Prudence's room and the clothes and items that had been strewn around. Who would have robbed the woman, and of what? It made no sense, especially given the lockdown of the floor. Another juror wouldn't risk stealing something from the woman because they'd be found out right away.

No, this wasn't some simple robbery. Someone had to either be looking for something or looking to use Prudence as a distraction. She quickly glanced back toward the common room to see if someone was trying to use the phone or sneak out of the building. She saw no one in that area.

"Do you know what might be missing?" Cindy asked, turning back to Prudence.

The woman glared at her. "How should I know?" she screeched. "I just got out of the shower. I haven't had time to take inventory."

Cindy took a deep breath. "What would a thief want to take of yours? Did you have anything valuable?"

"Like I'm going to tell you if I have valuables in my room," Prudence snapped.

The police officer had finished checking the room and had holstered his weapon. He stepped forward. “Ma’am, try to calm down.”

Apparently that was the exact wrong thing he could have said.

“You try calming down!” Prudence shrieked. “Your life hasn’t been turned completely upside down. Your privacy hasn’t been violated. I’m not the one on trial, you know. It’s that murdering piece of filth. The sooner we convict him, the sooner this nightmare can end.”

Ezra stepped forward, pushing slightly past Cindy to do so.

“This has been tough on all of us,” he said, voice soothing. “You’re going to be okay. You’re going to get through this because you are a strong, principled woman. And you are not alone. We are here with you.”

Ezra’s voice had a nearly hypnotic quality to it and Cindy found herself nodding as he spoke. It was a bit comical, actually, given that she didn’t think that Prudence was either strong or principled.

“Now, get dressed and help the officer figure out what was taken,” Ezra continued.

He was good. He even had Prudence nodding in agreement now.

A second officer appeared and he shepherded them all back to the common area. As Cindy took a seat on one of the couches she couldn’t help but think that surely this whole charade would be coming to an end any minute.

She was so sure of it that twenty minutes later when an officer announced that they’d be leaving for the courthouse soon she couldn’t hide her surprise.

She glanced around the group. “Where’s Jordan?” she asked, even though she already knew the answer.

“He had the stomach flu and went to the hospital earlier this morning,” the officer said. “He’s going to be just fine, but our other alternate juror will be required to step in.”

Lilian cursed, clearly not happy about it.

Cindy’s mind was racing. If they were moving forward then there must still be a problem. Maybe Jordan wasn’t the killer. That wouldn’t surprise her, especially in light of the most recent development. After all, he’d been in police custody when someone had searched Prudence’s room.

Cindy couldn’t shake the feeling that if she just knew what the perpetrator had been looking for she’d be able to figure out who it was. A minute later, though, they were being escorted down to the garage and the waiting cars. Cindy wished she’d had a chance to fill Jeremiah in, but she guessed he’d find out soon enough.

~

Jeremiah was relieved that the commotion down the hall hadn’t resulted in the police insisting on a room inspection. As it was things were already chaotic enough. He had been able to glean a lot about what was going on, though, by listening closely at the door. He’d even heard Prudence saying that she couldn’t figure out what the thieves might have taken.

He wasn’t sure if she was lying, she was too rattled to think straight, or the whole thing really had been just another diversion. Prudence would have been an easy target, guaranteed to cause quite a commotion just as she had. If, however, he and Cindy were right in their estimation that the killer was most likely in one of the rooms on this side of the hotel it wasn't the best choice. If the killer was on this side of the hotel and needed a diversion he would have been better served by one at the other end of the floor. It was possible that he hadn't been able to orchestrate that without raising the suspicions of the officer on duty in the common room.

When he knew the coast was clear he eased out of Cindy's room and down the hall. As much as he wanted to inspect Prudence's room, he knew he had to get out of there. He had work he needed to do back at the synagogue preparing for the next week.

~

Mark stood, staring out the window down at much of the city. He was on the fourteenth floor of a building, sitting in the main office of the newspaper waiting for the editor-in-chief to show up. His patience was growing thin and he was half a second away from getting the man's home address and going to his house to personally drag his butt out of bed.

His phone rang. Jeremiah was calling and he braced himself as he answered.

"Hello?"

"Good morning," Jeremiah said.

"Not from my perspective," Mark growled.

"I take it Jordan wasn't the killer?"

"Probably not."

"Have your people told you yet about the incident this morning?" Jeremiah asked.

"What incident?" Mark asked, glancing over at Liam.

"Apparently while she was in the shower someone broke into Prudence's room and went through her things."

"The mayor's wife?"

"Yes."

"What were they looking for?" Mark asked.

"Your guess is as good as mine."

"I seriously doubt that given that I don't even have a guess."

Jeremiah chuckled. "It's possible she was just being used as another distraction."

"I guess so."

"Otherwise I'd have to guess that whoever was in her room was looking for something specific to her."

"You mean like something valuable?"

"Perhaps," Jeremiah said. "Or something they could use to blackmail her."

"Maybe our mystery reporter was trying to get dirt on her," Mark mused.

"Mystery reporter?" Jeremiah asked.

"Yeah. I'm guessing you haven't seen the morning paper. Someone on the inside is either leaking information to a reporter or is a reporter."

"Oh wonderful," Jeremiah said.

"Tell me about it. We're hoping to find out who this person is here shortly."

"Good luck."

"Thanks."

"I'm heading into work," Jeremiah said. "You know how to reach me if you need me."

"Hopefully I won't. If I do we're all in trouble," Mark said with a sigh.

He ended the call and filled Liam in.

"We need to get this information now," Liam said.

"Tell me about it," Mark said, standing up and approaching the receptionist.

She glanced up at him with a frown.

"I need to know your editor's cell phone number and home address. Now."

"What seems to be the trouble?" someone asked behind him.

Mark turned around and saw a tall man with graying hair approaching, sipping a cup of overpriced coffee.

"Are you the editor?" Mark asked.

"I am. You can call me Bruce."

Mark flashed his badge. "I'm Detective Mark Walters. This is my partner, Liam. We need to speak with you immediately."

"Okay, let's talk in my office," the man said.

Mark noticed that the man didn't seem terribly surprised to have detectives visiting him. If he was smart he knew what was coming.

They followed him to his office and a minute later they were all sitting down.

"What can I do for you gentlemen?"

"You can help us solve a problem," Mark said. "We need to speak with one of your reporters, Felix Hoskins."

"I'm afraid Felix isn't in the office right now," Bruce said.

"When do you expect him in?" Liam asked.

"I really couldn't say. You know these young reporters, always hungry, always in the field tracking down stories," Bruce said dismissively.

"Then you can give us his address and phone number and we'll track him down," Mark said.

"You know, I'd love to help, but unfortunately we had a computer crash a couple of days ago and it wiped out our personnel files. It's going to take us a few weeks to recover all the data."

Mark's temper began to slip. Bruce knew what was going on and he was covering for his reporter so that he could grab more headlines while he could. He leaned forward. "Surely you have some paper files."

"We might have some old off-site archives, and I'd be happy to get my people searching through them if you could provide me with a warrant, Detectives."

"Felix is in a lot of trouble," Liam said. "A smart man like you might want to protect himself so you don't go down with him."

"Why, Detectives, whatever are you talking about?" Bruce asked, eyes wide. "I am aware of no wrong doing on the part of any of my staff. We adhere to the highest ethical standards."

"Cut the crap," Mark growled. "You know your boy is engaged in jury tampering at the very least. And trust me, when we find him you'll have nowhere to hide."

"Then it appears we have nothing left to discuss. Good day," Bruce said with a fake smile fixed in place.

Mark wanted nothing more than to smack that look off of the man's face. He barely managed to control himself, though. He stood and exited the office without another word. Liam followed.

They crossed to the elevator and Mark punched the button, wishing it was Bruce he was jabbing. The elevator, which had to be the slowest in all Pine Springs, arrived nearly a minute later, its doors creaking open. Mark and

Liam had stepped in and the doors were starting to close when a young woman scurried forward.

"Hold the door!"

Liam put his hand out and caught the door, allowing the young woman to slip inside.

"Thank you," she said.

The doors slid closed and the elevator began lumbering downward.

"You know what I hate?" she asked.

"What?" Mark asked, glancing quickly at Liam.

"I hate people that think they can break the rules and get away with it. You know, those guys who are always coloring outside the lines and yet never seem to get caught so they just get worse and worse. You know?"

"It's not fair," Mark said.

"No, it's not," she said, continuing to stare fixedly ahead at the elevator doors. "And then some people obey the rules, do everything right, and get screwed over by those cheaters."

"It's a crime, really," Liam said.

"It is. You know how long I've waited to get a front page article? You know how long I've paid my dues?"

"Too long," Mark said, sensing that she was leading to something.

"Exactly. I had a great story. I researched for four months. It was supposed to be my first front page story. It was supposed to print this morning," anger and bitterness colored her tone.

"It's a shame that it didn't happen. I bet it was a great story," Liam said.

"It was. An important story."

They were almost to the lobby.

"Instead they ran a story by a jerk who doesn't care who he hurts when he's trying to get himself headlines." She shifted a stack of papers in her arms and a photograph fell onto the floor of the elevator.

Mark stooped and picked it up, standing just as the elevator opened.

"Good luck finding what you're looking for," she said quietly before hurrying out of the elevator.

Mark stared at the picture he was holding. The caption below it read Felix Hoskins. The man smiling at him with the smug grin was familiar to him, but not as Felix. Mark was staring at a picture of one of the jurors.

21

Cindy was sitting in the jury box trying to watch the prosecuting attorney and the witness he was questioning. Her eyes kept drifting to Jason Todd, though. The man still gave her chills every time she looked at him. She couldn't help but feel that everyone was wasting their time. This whole thing was going to end up in a mistrial anyway. She just hoped that the next jury who took over could get the job done.

And as much as she wanted to try the case exclusively on its merits, she couldn't help but hope that Todd was convicted and sent away for a long, long time. The man suddenly swiveled his head and stared right at her. This time she didn't look away. She held his gaze wanting him to know that she wasn't afraid, that she knew he was a terrible man, and that she hoped he was going to prison for the rest of his life.

He finally looked away and she forced herself to turn and give her attention to the witness. Cassidy Todd's best friend was testifying.

"How would you describe the relationship between Cassidy and the accused?" the attorney asked.

"It was terrible. They argued all the time. Jason didn't care who was around or who heard him. He said the most awful things. I urged her to leave him. She would just shrug it off and say that things would get better. That she'd lived through worse. She said that up to the week before her death."

Cindy shuddered, wondering what had been worse in Cassidy's past.

"What happened then?" the attorney asked.

"She called me up one morning after he'd left for work, sobbing. She'd said she'd had enough. He'd done something awful to her at a dinner party they'd been hosting the night before, but she wouldn't tell me what it was. She said she was going to see a divorce attorney and end things."

"Do you know who might have been at the dinner party?"

"No. It's usually people from Jason's work, but she didn't say any names."

The attorney asked her a few more questions. After the conversation with Jeremiah that morning, the story of Esther was on Cindy's mind. She couldn't help but think about how the chance for Esther to save her people had come about because of the king becoming angry with his wife, Queen Vashti, at a party.

When the woman had finished testifying, an attorney was called to the stand. He swore under oath that Cassidy Todd had retained his services three days before her death for the purpose of divorcing her husband. He described her as being very fearful. Given the history of abuse he had recommended that they file a restraining order against Jason Todd for the duration of the proceedings. She had hesitated to do so, though, because she wasn't quite ready to inform him that she wanted a divorce.

He did have pictures he had taken of Cassidy the day she came to see him showing bruises on several parts of her body. When the pictures were displayed, Tara gave a little cry and then buried her head in her hands, refusing to look more closely at them.

A bailiff approached the judge while the attorney was displaying the pictures and whispered something to him which made the judge frown. As soon as the attorney had finished showing the pictures the judge banged his gavel, clearly surprising both attorneys.

"We're going to break now for lunch. Bailiff, please escort the jurors to their room."

Something unusual had happened and Cindy was willing to bet that it had everything to do with Mark. Maybe the whole thing was finally going to be over, though she was sure Jordan couldn't be the culprit.

As they left the courtroom and walked down the hallway leading to the jury break room, Cindy was at the back of the group with Tanner and Joyce just in front of her. She was walking slowly, wondering exactly what was about to happen.

The bailiff opened the door and people began to walk inside. When she got close she saw that Mark and Liam were already in the room, faces stony looking. *They are here for the real killer*, she realized.

Joyce stepped into the room, but Tanner froze on the threshold. Suddenly he spun and shoved Cindy hard. She barely kept her feet as he sprinted down the hallway.

"Get him!" Mark roared.

Without thinking Cindy started sprinting after him. The bailiff flashed past her a few steps later, giving chase for all he was worth. Moments later Liam passed her as well. He was lightning fast and he passed the bailiff a second later and then was on top of Tanner. He grabbed the fleeing man and shoved him down onto the ground.

Mark came to a halt next to Cindy a couple of feet away.

"Felix Hoskins?" Liam asked.

Tanner sighed. "Yes, that's me," he said.

"You're under arrest. You have the right to remain silent…"

Cindy listened as Liam read the man his rights. When Liam was finished she turned to Mark. "How did you figure out who it was?" she asked.

"Felix here is a reporter it turns out. He published an article on the front page of the paper this morning with information about the trial only an insider could have had. Well, we found out that Tanner is just the name he stole and was using so that he could get the scoop on everyone else."

"I'd do it again, too," Felix said defiantly. "It wasn't even hard. I was hoping to get a feel for the attorneys, the questions they were asking, the potential jurors. I honestly never thought I'd make it onto the jury, but when I did I knew I couldn't stop. I had a golden opportunity that I could not pass up."

"Even if you were breaking the law," Cindy said coldly.

"Hey, who was I hurting?"

"For starters, the three guys you killed," Liam said.

"Wait, what?" Felix asked.

"The real Tanner, whose jury summons you stole after you killed him. Isaac Bernstein, the reporter who recognized you the first day of the trial and would have outed you. And, finally, you killed Wyatt, probably because he knew who you were as well. Either that or you were just hoping to add more drama to the whole story so you could get even more fame," Mark said.

"Wait. I didn't kill anyone," Felix said, his tone suddenly changed from arrogant to confused and a bit frightened. "Tanner, I paid him two hundred bucks to give me his jury summons. I know a guy who was able to help me out with a fake id. Yeah, Isaac knew me and was pissed, but I had nothing to do with him having a heart attack. And Wyatt…wait, Wyatt's actually dead? I thought he'd just skipped out. I wrote the article I did to sensationalize things a bit, but you're telling me he's actually dead? Where? How?"

Cindy was beginning to have a bad feeling in her gut. Felix wasn't the killer. She turned and headed back to the jury room. If Felix wasn't the killer that meant the real killer was still among the other jurors. And now he'd know that the police were looking for him.

Carson.

That was the name that popped into her mind. He'd had that cell and watch the first day of the trial. He could have used them to orchestrate the attack outside the courtroom that first morning. But why? What would he have hoped to gain from that?

She stepped into the jury room and every head swiveled toward her.

"What's happening out there?" Carson asked.

Cindy took a deep breath. "The police are trying to capture a killer."

"Who?" Joyce asked.

Cindy let her eyes scan the room, lingering on each face. "One of us."

~

Mark was starting to get an itch in the back of his mind. Something was wrong. Felix was guilty of half a dozen things, most of them serious, but Mark was seriously rethinking Felix's potential role as a murderer. Felix, at least, seemed scared enough that he was running his mouth off without bothering to wait for a lawyer.

"Look, I pretended to be someone I wasn't, yes. I even set off the fire alarm so that I had a chance to use the phone and call in my story."

"Who did you call?"

"The editor-in-chief."

"Did he know what you were doing?" Liam asked.

"Of course," Felix said.

Mark glanced at Liam. That was one victory. They could go after that smug jerk now.

"What else?" Mark asked.

"I went through Prudence's room this morning while she was in the shower."

"Why? What were you looking for?" Liam asked.

"I saw some guy sneak out of her room in the middle of the night. I thought maybe she was having an affair or at least some sort of secret dealings with one of the other jurors or one of the cops. I broke in and went through her things, hoping to find a clue to the mystery man's identity. I mean, the mayor's wife having an affair and while sequestered for jury duty? That's a story that's just too good to pass up, you know?"

"And what did you find?" Mark pressed.

"Nothing. And she took like a three second shower which I wasn't expecting. I heard the water turn off and I panicked. I knew I didn't have time to put things back."

"So you made a mess instead."

"Like I said, I panicked. I thought she'd blame someone looking for valuables or something."

"The jury summons you bought off the real Tanner, is it actually at your house?" Mark asked.

"Yes."

They had been working under the assumption that the killer would have a jury summons with a torn corner. It should be easy to get a warrant to search Felix's place and see what condition Tanner's jury summons was in.

"The man you bought the jury summons from, where is he?" Mark asked.

"On vacation. That's why he was so eager to unload it. He won't be back for a couple of weeks."

"Convenient," Liam muttered.

"Look, I swear it's the truth!"

Mark was afraid the man was telling the truth. He turned to glance at Cindy. She wasn't there.

"Where's Cindy?" Mark turned to ask Liam.

His partner shrugged. "I don't know, maybe she went back to the jury room?"

Mark's blood ran cold. He looked around. The bailiff was missing as well.

~

Jeremiah had just finished making the last of a dozen calls to verify and nail down things for the Purim carnival coming up in a few days. He really was going to have to talk to those who controlled the purse strings about giving Marie a raise. Whatever she was making, it wasn't enough.

At least during all the chaos Mark had come through. The coroner had been allowing a couple of Jewish officers to sit with Isaac's body until he released it. That was a comfort to Marie, especially given that it meant they could keep an eye on the coroner and make sure that everything he did was as minimally invasive as possible. Desecration of a body was not taken lightly in Jewish culture.

He stood up to stretch his legs for a minute, having been hunched over Marie's desk for the last couple of hours. He glanced at the clock on the wall. It was only eleven in the morning, but it felt like it was later. Cindy and the other jurors wouldn't likely be on their lunch break yet.

He thought about calling Mark to see if he'd made any progress in finding the killer. He started to pull his phone out of his pocket and then froze.

Something wasn't right.

He didn't know how he knew, but he just did. Every time he'd ever had that feeling in his life it had been accurate, G-d trying to tell him something. He had learned to pay attention.

Which was why seconds later he had sprinted to his car, got inside, and was speeding toward the courthouse. He prayed as he drove. It was the best thing he could do and it also helped calm and focus him.

There was a huge crowd milling around outside when he got to the courthouse, all buzzing with some sort of excitement. He raced up the steps to the front doors. They were locked and he couldn't see any guards in sight. Not good.

He sprinted down the side of the building, looking for an emergency exit of some sort. He finally found one and was able after a few seconds work to get it open. He made it inside and followed the sounds of shouting.

He saw a couple guards first, fear and confusion on their faces. Then he saw some of the jurors scattering into a hallway. Past them Mark and Liam were standing, guns drawn and staring fixedly at something inside a room.

"Get back!" he heard someone roar from inside the room.

The jurors fled down the hall past him, heading for the locked front doors. The guards backpedalled and Mark and Liam stood their ground.

Slowly he saw two pairs of feet inching forward from inside the room. A moment later he zeroed in on Carson's face. The man was scared, face flushed. "I didn't kill anyone!" he yelled.

"Put down the gun and we'll talk about that!" Mark ordered.

Jeremiah just stared in horror. Carson did indeed have a gun and a hostage. He had his left arm wrapped around the woman's chest and in his right hand was a gun that he had aimed at her temple.

Carson had Cindy.

22

Cindy locked eyes with Jeremiah. Carson had freaked out and when the bailiff came he had knocked the man out and taken his gun.

"I didn't kill anyone!" he was shouting.

Carson moved the gun, making as though he was going to point it at someone else.

Cindy stepped down on his instep and rammed her elbow into his stomach. Carson's grip loosened and she spun away from him just as Liam sprang forward and knocked the gun from his hand. Cindy ran to Jeremiah who enfolded her in a tight embrace. Her heart was thundering in her chest, and she closed her eyes for a moment, just breathing in his scent and feeling herself begin to calm.

Within moments Carson was in handcuffs.

"I didn't kill anyone," he protested again.

"Then what did you do?" Mark asked.

"I gave inside information to a guy in Vegas to rig the betting on the trial. I had no choice. I'm into this guy for a lot of money and it was the only option he gave me for squaring my debt. You don't mess with these guys. That's why I smuggled the phone and the watch into the trial. When they were confiscated I had to get creative. He saw me," Carson said, pointing to Jeremiah. "The night the fire alarm went off I waited until I was sure everyone had to be out of the building, then I went out to use the phone to call in my information. He chased me. I got away and grabbed a towel by the pool so I could pretend I'd been in the shower when I joined everyone outside."

"I knew that was a pool towel!" Cindy exclaimed.

Jeremiah nodded. "You were right."

"I admit it, I passed information that could be used to rig the betting, but I never hurt anyone."

~

Jeremiah believed Carson. While the man was continuing to talk, Jeremiah turned, his eyes skimming the other jurors. He saw looks of confusion, fear, anxiety. And then he saw what he was looking for. There was one juror who was calmly watching everything that was transpiring.

He was the man who had killed Wyatt and disposed of his body in such an efficient manner. He was the one who had poisoned and killed Marie's brother in a crowd full of people then managed to give Jeremiah the slip. The man who dressed like a blue-collar worker but who had no calluses on his hands. And, unless Jeremiah was seriously mistaken, the man was wearing a gun concealed in a holster strapped to his calf, most likely one made of porcelain that wouldn't have been picked up by the metal detectors.

"What is it? Who are you looking at?" Cindy whispered.

"Mike," Jeremiah said, launching himself forward as he said it.

The other man saw him move, had clearly anticipated it, and reached down toward his leg. Jeremiah dove to the ground, sliding and slamming into Mike, toppling him over as they both struggled to be the first to reach his gun. All around them there was shouting as the two men grappled together, each trying to gain the upper hand.

After a moment Jeremiah gave up on trying to grab the gun and instead grabbed and twisted Mike's wrist, snapping the bone. The other man howled in pain even as he gouged at Jeremiah's eyes with his good hand.

Jeremiah twisted his head and flipped his body, breaking Mike's leg in the process. He would break the man a piece at a time if he had to. There was a thud and suddenly Mike stopped struggling, his whole body going limp. Jeremiah turned and saw that there was blood trickling from a cut on Mike's scalp. Standing above him, holding a fire extinguisher in her hands, was Cindy.

He blinked up at her in surprise and she gave him a weak smile. Mark scrambled forward and hastily cuffed the unconscious man. "What the heck just happened?" he demanded as he stood up.

"I think you'll find that this is your killer," Jeremiah said, getting up as well.

Mark looked from Mike to Carson to Felix. "How many bad guys are we dealing with?" he asked, shaking his head.

"At least one more. I'm pretty sure someone hired this guy," Jeremiah said, indicating Mike.

"To do what, exactly?"

"Tamper with the jury would be my guess. Make sure things swung a certain way."

"But which way?" Mark asked.

"Wyatt was eager to convict and go home, so I'm guessing this guy was working for Todd," Cindy piped up. "He could have seen that there was no way he could sway Wyatt to come over to his side, so he got rid of him in favor of one of the alternates."

"It's true," Carson spoke up from his spot on the floor.

"How do you know that?" Mark asked.

"He talked to me. He was subtle, I'll give him that, but he made it clear he knew that I was passing information on to a man I owed a lot of money to in Vegas. He said that no one had to know, but he'd be counting on my vote when the time came. I'm willing to testify to that, particularly if it will help me out."

"Would you be willing to testify against the guy in Vegas, too?" Liam asked.

Carson dropped his head and then slowly nodded.

"Did Mike here ever say anything about Todd directly?" Mark asked.

"No," Carson said. "I'm sorry."

Mark looked around at the other jurors. "Anyone else have anything to add?"

Joyce raised her hand. "He seemed like such a nice young man. We talked a little and he said that he always thought it was important to give people the benefit of the doubt. I agreed with him. I told him that I was afraid of sending an innocent man to prison. He didn't threaten me, he just talked to me for a minute or two the other day."

Mark nodded his head. "Sounds like he was making his way through the jurors, making sure he could get them in his pocket."

Cindy frowned. "He did seem nice, and he saved me from a nasty fall down the stairs during the fire alarm."

"He was engendering trust," Jeremiah said softly. "So you'd be inclined to trust him as a person and, therefore, his opinion."

"Someone slipped a note under my door last night," Felix spoke up suddenly. "It said that they knew who I was and that I was playing a dangerous game and that it would be bad for me if the police found out."

"He could have been getting ready to blackmail you into voting his way," Cindy said.

"Which could explain him killing Isaac so that Isaac couldn't blow Felix's cover," Jeremiah mused.

"But who pushed the protestor out in front of the car?" Mark asked. "That couldn't have been any of the three of them."

"An accomplice?" Cindy asked.

Mike groaned and slowly opened his eyes.

Mark was instantly next to him, face inches from the downed man.

"Okay, tell us the truth. Did Todd hire you to rig the jury in his favor?"

Mike began to laugh. "You couldn't be more wrong."

"What do you mean?" Mark asked.

"The person who hired me wanted Todd free so they could kill him. I'll speak with my lawyer now."

Mark stood up, frustration clear on his face. "Three criminals in handcuffs and we've still got one heck of a mess," he said.

~

Three days later they were still sorting the whole mess out. Mark was exhausted. They hadn't gotten anything more out of the guy who had been masquerading as Mike. At least they knew that Mike was the guy who'd been killed in the alley for his jury summons. The fake Mike, whatever his name was, had stolen the corner of Jordan's summons and then ripped his up and taped it back together with the corner once he'd realized his had been damaged in the scuffle with its owner.

The entire debacle had made national news and the mistrial that resulted had frustrated a great many people. Personally he suspected that Todd should be grateful for the reprieve since whoever wanted him dead seemed unwilling or unable to accomplish that while the man was in police custody.

A new venue for the trial had yet to be set, but given everything that had happened Mark was reasonably sure Pine Springs would be off the hook. He still thought Todd was guilty and ultimately hoped that the man spent the rest of his life in a jail cell. He would just be glad to have the whole circus moved to someone else's jurisdiction, though.

It was still unclear who had caused the car accident. Maybe it would come out at one of the other trials that would be happening. Felix had given them enough on his editor's collaboration that they'd be able to take both men down. Same with Carson and his Vegas connections. Liam's cousin seemed very pleased about that. Mark had been careful not to make any more wisecracks about that family connection.

Now it was Monday late morning and he was heading home for a few well-deserved days off with Traci and the twins. He was planning on turning his phone off when he got there. If the world came to an end he was sure the news would reach him eventually. Liam had spent the afternoon pacing and staring at the clock. He had a date with Rebecca who was officially off the suspect list.

There were questions unanswered, things undone, but Mark was content to leave those questions and things to someone else. He had enough unsolved mysteries of his own to worry about these.

~

Cindy hesitated before knocking on the door. She was standing on Marie's porch. She had come by on her lunch hour and brought food for the family. They had buried Marie's brother the day before and it was her understanding that the woman would be sitting Shiva, which required others to do things for her. When someone was sitting Shiva they were supposed to just reflect on the person they had lost and not do any work of any kind. That was why Cindy had brought some food for the family. It felt wrong not to pay her respects.

Now that she was here, though, she was questioning her judgment. Marie didn't like her. Maybe seeing her would just upset the poor woman more. Still, Marie was Jeremiah's secretary and she and Cindy were going to have more and more dealings with each other as time went on. Perhaps this could be the first step toward making peace.

She knocked and a minute later Marie's husband answered the door. He smiled when he saw her. "It's good of you to come, although I'm surprised," he said.

"You're not the only one," Cindy said with a shaky laugh, handing him the basket of food.

"Thank you, come in, please."

He ushered her inside.

Marie was in the family room, sitting on a chair. Her clothes were rent and Cindy had a hitch in her throat as she remembered Jeremiah rending his shirt for his family back in Israel. She looked tired and deeply distressed.

"Go over and say something," her husband urged quietly.

There was a chair next to Marie and Cindy walked over slowly and sat down. "I'm sorry for your loss," she muttered.

Marie turned to look at her, surprise in her eyes. "Thank you."

"Is there anything I can do?" Cindy asked, at a loss as to what else to say.

Marie stared at her for several seconds, looking at her, really studying her. Then she sighed.

"I'm worried about Jeremiah having to handle Purim," Marie confessed. "It's the last thing I should be thinking about, but it's like I can't let it go and just focus on my brother like I need to."

Cindy hesitated then reached out and put a hand on Marie's arm. "I had an idea about that, but I haven't had a chance to share it with Jeremiah."

"What is it?" Marie asked.

"He said the big problem was getting people to let the shuttles take them home before they passed out."

"That's true," Marie said with a deep sigh.

"It's my understanding that giving gifts is a part of the holiday. I was thinking that since sunset is when the celebration is supposed to end that about an hour before sunset he could make an announcement that he's hidden special gifts in the yards of a couple of attendees but that if they don't find them by sunset he's going to go around and take them back. Make it a game with a couple of prizes that would motivate people to go home and really look. Then, if they pass out, they do it on their own lawns."

Marie stared at her for several seconds and Cindy was beginning to regret sharing her idea with her. Suddenly Marie reached out and grabbed Cindy, kissing each of her cheeks. When she pulled back tears were streaming down Marie's face.

"What's wrong?" Cindy asked in alarm.

Marie's lips were quivering as she smiled. "I used to play at making scavenger hunts with my brother, Isaac, when we were children. He would have loved this idea."

"I'm glad," Cindy said, suddenly choked up.

"I'm not happy that you and Jeremiah are getting married since you do not share the same faith. But I believe now that you will be a help to him and not a hindrance in his work. Thank you. It is a wonderful idea."

Marie took a deep breath and it seemed as if her whole body suddenly slumped. She buried her head in her hands and began to sob. Cindy didn't know what to do so she began to rub Marie's back, praying silently for the other woman.

When Cindy finally left half an hour later she felt lighter, as though a burden had been lifted. Marie and she had made progress. There was hope for that relationship.

She headed back to church, thinking about all the things that she had to get done that afternoon. The moment she walked into the office, though, Geanie turned and looked at her. "Pastor Ben wants to see you in his office," she said.

"What about?"

"He wouldn't say, but I didn't like his tone," Geanie said.

"Okay, well let's see what the latest crisis is," Cindy said.

A minute later she was sitting down in the pastor's office. He had been there several months now, but they still hadn't had a chance to spend much time together.

She smiled as she sat down across from him. He didn't return the look. "I hear you've had a busy week."

"You could say that," she said with a short laugh.

He still didn't smile and she started to get a bad feeling in the pit of her stomach.

"What is it?" she asked.

"Cindy, as your spiritual leader I feel it imperative that I give you spiritual correction when it becomes obvious that you need it."

"What?" she asked, her stomach twisting into a tight knot. She started to feel a bit queasy. No one had ever said something like that to her.

"You're making a huge mistake, yoking yourself with the rabbi. It's not good for you and it's not good for this church given that you are a very visible part of its administration. I'm not the only one who feels this way. Many of us are concerned."

"I know that Jeremiah and I have different faiths, but we're working through how to deal with that," she said. It wasn't like these thoughts hadn't been with her ever since she and Jeremiah met.

"No, you're not. You're caving. And I can't have that. I've already talked to him and he's just as stubborn about this as you. He is not for you. Not for the church secretary. You need to provide an example. You need to repent and you need to break up with him."

Cindy's blood seemed to turn to ice. "No."

He leaned across the desk, jabbing a finger at her. "I don't think I'm making myself clear."

She stood, her legs shaking beneath her. "Then let me make myself clear. I am not in this blindly. I know where God has led me even though I don't know why. If you can't accept that, then I quit."

He leaned back in his chair and laced his fingers in front of him. "So be it."

She turned and somehow made her way out of his office and back into the main office. So many emotions were exploding inside her that she couldn't even keep track of them. Geanie took one look at her and leaped up from her desk. She came forward and wrapped her arms around her.

"What's wrong?" Geanie asked.

Cindy buried her head in her friend's shoulder as tears began to fall. "I just quit my job."

She barely heard Geanie whisper, "Oh no!" before the other woman was sobbing, too.

Debbie Viguié is the New York Times Bestselling author of more than three dozen novels including the *Wicked* series, the *Crusade* series and the *Wolf Springs Chronicles* series co-authored with Nancy Holder. Debbie also writes thrillers including *The Psalm 23 Mysteries,* the *Kiss* trilogy, and the *Witch Hunt* trilogy. She is busy working on a new Robin Hood series with co-author James R. Tuck. When Debbie isn't busy writing she enjoys spending time with her husband, Scott, visiting theme parks. They live in Florida with their cat, Schrödinger.

CPSIA information can be obtained
at www.ICGtesting.com
Printed in the USA
LVHW010006071222
734695LV00004B/332

9 780990 697145